Out of Time

Alex got to his feet and looked Caroline in the eye. "One hundred percent of your time is wrapped up in you. I was willing to take second place because I could see you needed all the support you could get, but I'm not willing to wait around forever. Just remember that. I'm a person, too, Caroline. I have feelings of my own." He turned, walked to the front door, and shut it quietly behind him.

Caroline stood staring down the empty hallway as if she were made of stone. In the months they had been dating, she and Alex had never before had a real fight. And this one was all her fault.

I deserve to lose him, she thought, feeling despair settling on her. *I've been so wrapped up in my own problems, that I haven't had time to think of anyone else. Why did I say such terrible things to him?*

Other books in the **SUGAR & SPICE** series:

This page has been composed using our
IMP (Interactive Make-up Program)/QPO (Quadex Pagination Option)

Janet Quin-Harkin's

Sugar & Spice

The Last Dance

IVY BOOKS • NEW YORK

Ivy Books
Published by Ballantine Books

Copyright © 1987 by Butterfield Press, Inc. & Janet Quin-Harkin

Produced by Butterfield Press, Inc.
133 Fifth Avenue
New York, New York 10003

Library of Congress Catalog Card Number:87-90787

ISBN 0-8041-0033-0

Manufactured in the United States of America

First Edition: July 1987

Chapter 1

"I can't believe it," Caroline Kirby said with a contented sigh. She ran her hands through her blond shoulder-length hair. It felt funny hanging freely around her face and not tied back in her usual ballet-school braid. "A whole evening to ourselves with nothing special to do," she said, turning to look at her boyfriend Alex, who was sitting beside her.

Alex smiled at her, his dark eyes lighting up his face. He slid his arm around Caroline's shoulders and pulled her closer to him on the white wicker porch seat. "Maybe I should record this in my diary," he agreed. "Caroline and I finally had a free evening together. She had no ballet practice, no art committee meeting, no meeting to save the old houses, save the whales, save the seals,

1

save the parks, no concert to go to—"

"And Alex had no soccer practice." Caroline interrupted. "I'm not the only one with a hectic lifestyle, you know."

"True," Alex agreed, "but mine is just normally hectic for the active, intelligent high school junior. Your schedule is for crazy people!"

Caroline sighed. "It does seem that way sometimes, doesn't it? Sometimes I watch other kids strolling out of school as if they had all the time in the world, and I ask myself why I'm stuck with a schedule that only gives me five minutes per day to breathe."

"Because you are going to end up the world's most famous ballerina, and when you're on stage I'll be able to dig people in the ribs and tell them that I used to know you way back when."

Caroline wriggled sideways in the seat to look at Alex, her ice-blue eyes suddenly serious. "I find that hard to imagine," she said. "I try to think about myself as a famous ballerina and I just can't picture it. And I wouldn't ever want to lose touch with all my friends either. If I'm ever famous, promise that you'll still be my friend."

"If you promise to give me free tickets to your ballets," Alex replied jokingly.

Caroline still didn't smile. "Don't you get scared thinking about the future, Alex?" she asked.

"Not me," Alex said. "There are too many years before I have to start getting scared. There's no sense in panicking before it's necessary. I know I want to be an engineer, and I want to get into a campus of the University of California. My grades should be good enough for that, so I don't really have to start worrying until I'm looking for a job and my parents throw me out." He gave her a big grin. "Of course, my mother does threaten to throw me out fairly often when she sees the state of my room, so maybe I should start worrying."

"I worry," Caroline said solemnly.

Alex nodded. "Well, you're a born worrier, aren't you? If the sun is shining when you wake up, you worry that it might rain tomorrow."

"I'm not as bad as that," Caroline said, "but I do worry about living up to what everyone expects of me."

Alex stretched, and the wicker creaked and groaned. "You made a big mistake, being an only child," he said. "Having an older brother makes it much easier. There's not much I could do now that he hasn't already done. But parents always expect the worst!"

Caroline laughed. "Mine always expect me to be perfect."

Alex looked at her tenderly. "And you are," he whispered, leaning forward to kiss her gently on the tip of her nose.

Caroline blushed with pleasure and embarrassment. "You're pretty nice yourself," she said.

"So now that we've decided we're the two best people ever created, what are we going to do with a precious free evening?" Alex asked.

Caroline snuggled against him. "Just sitting here looking at the view sounds good to me," she replied. Her eyes took in the pastel-covered hills of San Francisco, stretching down to the sparkling blue water of the bay dotted with sailboats, the dramatic swing of the Golden Gate Bridge, and the curve of the bare hills beyond. "I have this wonderful view right out of my windows, and I'm usually too busy to notice it. I feel guilty sometimes when I'm rushing down the hill and I don't even notice the sailboats out in the bay."

Alex chuckled, and Caroline could feel his body laughing next to hers. "Only a champion worrier could feel guilty about not looking at a view!"

"I didn't mean it like that, Alex," Caroline said hastily. "But it does seem a shame to live in one of the most beautiful cities and not even notice."

"The view is nice," Alex agreed, "but in about half an hour the sun will go down and it will be cold out here. Do you want to sit here all evening and slowly turn blue? Let's go inside."

"It's so hard to find a place to be alone in my apartment these days," Caroline said. "Whenever I find a peaceful spot, Chrissy turns up."

"Is your cousin still bugging you?" Alex asked. "I thought you had things worked out pretty well with her by now."

"I do," Caroline said quickly, "and she really tries not to bug me. At least she's not acting like the little farm girl straight from Iowa anymore. In fact she's finally back to normal after her attempt to be the world's most sophisticated person. Thank heavens for that! She's not trying to cook pickled duck eggs or set fire to the pancakes anymore, or borrow all my best outfits to impress Hunter."

"Is that romance over, then?"

"All over," Caroline said, nodding. "Chrissy finally saw the light when Hunter wanted her to go to that houseboat in Sausalito with him. She liked him enough to change her personality, but not her down-home morals!"

"So she's back to good old Chrissy again, rushing through the house like a tornado?"

"Pretty much," Caroline agreed. "That girl has too much extra energy when she's not working on a farm. Since the art fair's over, she has nothing to do in the evenings."

"Take her along to your ballet classes," Alex suggested.

Caroline's eyes opened wide. "Are you kidding? Chrissy would make Madame commit suicide in half an hour. She'd question every command, and suggest better ways to do it, and chat with the male dancer while he tried to lift her. Besides, I'm in advanced classes. There's no way she could skip ten years of sweat and suffering to be in advanced ballet."

"Of course not," Alex said hastily. "Dumb idea. Anyway, why are we sitting here discussing your cousin when we're actually alone together?"

He pulled Caroline toward him. "Come to think of it, why are we discussing anything?" he whispered as his lips approached hers.

"I don't know," she whispered back, her eyes

teasing his. "Can you think of any other way to pass the time?"

"I have one good idea," he whispered before his lips finally met hers.

"Caroline, where are you?" Chrissy's powerful voice startled Caroline. She and Alex quickly broke apart as they heard her cousin yelling up the steps from the street below. "Are you home yet, Cara? I've got something I can't wait to show you!"

Alex grinned at Caroline while Chrissy ran up the steep steps two at a time. She looked as if she'd run all the way home. Her straw-blond hair had escaped from her headband, her normally healthy-looking cheeks were bright pink, and papers were threatening to escape from her book bag. She saw Caroline and Alex sitting together and her face lit up into an excited smile.

"Oh, you're both here. Terrific. Now I can show you both and see what you think—I tried it out for myself in the bathroom after school and I've been running it through in my head all the way home. Watch."

Before Alex or Caroline could say anything, Chrissy launched into a sort of Irish jig mixed with a square dance, to which she half sang, half hummed a little tune: "Oh, the farmer and the cowman should be friends." Here she hummed off-key, then repeated the line—clearly the only line of the song that she knew—and did the whole routine a few more times.

"Well?" she asked, breathing heavily as she

finished. "What do you think?"

Alex and Caroline both continued to stare.

"Very nice," Alex said politely.

"Is this some sort of fall ritual from Iowa that we don't know about?" Caroline asked cautiously. "Harvest festival dance or something?"

Chrissy looked at them blankly, then burst out laughing. "It's for *Oklahoma!*" she said.

"Oh," Caroline and Alex said together.

"Are you thinking of moving there?" Alex asked.

Chrissy laughed again. "*Oklahoma!* the play!" she said. "Didn't you guys listen to the bulletin at school today? Holy cow!"

"Oh, you mean that *Oklahoma!* is going to be the school musical this year," Caroline said, laughing with Chrissy. "I think I heard some kids talking about it in the hall today."

"They announced it on the bulletin," Chrissy said, perching herself on the arm of Caroline and Alex's porch seat, "and they said there are open tryouts tomorrow and the next day."

"So you thought you might try?" Caroline suggested.

"Seeing that I know more than any other person in school about farmers and cowmen, I thought I'd give it a shot," Chrissy replied. "Just for the dancing chorus. Do you reckon I've got a chance?"

"Sure you have," Caroline said. "It's only a high school musical after all, not Broadway. All the dancers will be people like you, with no real training."

"I've been trying to work out an audition dance," Chrissy said. "Do you think my hoedown thing would be right?"

"It looked fine," Caroline said. "I've seen the musicals at school. All the chorus has to do is stand in a line and hop around a little. You'd find it easy."

"Are you sure?" Chrissy asked. "Because I don't know any real dance steps, and I don't want to look like a fool."

"Chrissy, I've seen you move to music," Caroline said warmly. "You'd be as good as anyone there. Go for it, I say."

"Me, too," Alex said. "I bet it would be a lot of fun."

"And it would be kind of nice being back on a farm again," Chrissy said wistfully. "Even if it is only a fake farm. At least I'd get to wear overalls and ginghams and they'd have fake corn on stage. I think I will go for it. Will you coach me tonight, Cara?"

"Chrissy," Caroline said in a stern voice, "haven't I coached you enough? I've already been through the entire history of Western art, all the restaurants in San Francisco, every symphony ever written, and every major city in the world, just to get you in shape to date Hunter. Just dance naturally. You move well, you'll do fine."

"But what if the other kids all do ballet and stuff?"

"They won't," Caroline said. "Any serious dance

students couldn't afford the time to be in a school production. They'll all be cheerleaders and know how to do a few kicks, that's all."

"Maybe you'd just watch my routine and help me get it totally right?" Chrissy asked. "Just once through, maybe?"

Caroline sighed. "Okay. I'll watch your routine, but just once. For the first time all year I've got an evening alone with Alex, and I plan to make the most of it."

Chrissy flushed pink. "Gee, how dumb of me. I barged right in on you. I'm sorry. Well, I'm going upstairs to get my homework done. Then I'll practice my dance by myself in the bathroom, so don't worry if you hear thumps. I won't bother you again. Have a good evening." Then she bounded up the last two steps and disappeared in through the front door.

Alex turned to Caroline and grinned. "What were we saying about Chrissy being a tornado?" he asked.

Caroline stared after her cousin. "She's so enthusiastic about everything. Most people here think it's juvenile to act so excited, but Chrissy throws herself into everything she does. But I do have to confess, Alex, that it is sometimes a little overwhelming to be her roommate!" She gave a little sigh. "I suppose I had better help her with her routine, or I'll feel guilty about it."

Alex slipped his arm around her shoulder again. "Wouldn't you feel more guilty if you deserted me?" he whispered. "I need some of your famous coaching, too."

"What do you need coaching in, Alex?" she asked, her eyes teasing his.

"In memory," he whispered back. "I've forgotten what we were doing before Chrissy interrupted."

"Oh, that's easy," Caroline said, moving her face toward his. "I'll show you once, then I bet you get the hang of it!"

Chapter 2

Caroline was climbing back up the hill from dance class the next night when she saw Chrissy coming along the cross street toward her. This time Chrissy was not bouncing along with giant strides; she was walking about as slowly as she could walk, trailing her book bag beside her and staring down at the sidewalk.

"Chrissy!" Caroline called to her. "Have you been to tryouts? How did it go?"

Chrissy jumped as if waking up from a dream. As Caroline hurried over to join her, she could see instantly from her cousin's face that things had not gone well. "Not good, huh?" she asked. "What happened? Didn't you get picked?"

Chrissy gave her cousin a despairing glance. "It was awful, Cara," she said, pausing and letting her book bag sink to the sidewalk. "Talk about being psyched out!"

"Why? What happened?" Caroline asked. "I would have thought that your routine was one of the best there. What did the director say?"

"She didn't say anything to me," Chrissy said, picking up her bag and beginning to walk on slowly again.

"You mean she just turned you down and didn't even tell you why?" Caroline asked angrily.

Chrissy stared straight ahead of her. "She never got to see me dance," she said. "I chickened out at the last minute."

"Chrissy! What on earth made you do that?"

Chrissy sighed. "I didn't want to make a fool of myself, Cara. You've no idea how it was. There were all these girls in leotards on stage. I was just in my school clothes—they didn't say in the bulletin that we should wear leotards!"

"It really doesn't matter what you wear to auditions, Chrissy," Caroline said gently. "You should see what some of the kids wear to ballet tryouts—tattered old T-shirts tied up around their waists, or tights with huge holes in them— whatever feels comfortable."

"Maybe," Chrissy said cautiously. "But it didn't seem like that at school. It felt like everyone else was properly dressed except me. And there was this woman up on stage teaching them a special dance—a new dance, Cara, so my routine would have been wasted anyway—and she kept calling out things that I didn't understand—all these ballet words, I guess. She'd yell out shanay, shanay, and everyone would turn around. They all knew what she was talking about. I didn't want to be the only one who didn't know when to turn. I probably would've knocked the others off the stage, so I snuck out again."

"What a shame, Chrissy," Caroline said with understanding. "You were really excited about getting a part in the play."

"I know, I really was, but I didn't want to be laughed at."

"I'm sure nobody would laugh at you," Caroline said firmly. "And I bet you could have picked up the dance as quickly as anyone there, if you hadn't been frightened off by the words she was using."

"I didn't want to take that risk," Chrissy said. "Since I arrived here I've done so many things I thought were okay, and I had no idea why people were laughing at me. After a while that starts to get to you, Cara. I don't enjoy being laughed at."

"Nobody does," Caroline said. "Well, there are more tryouts tomorrow night, aren't there? I'll try and teach you some dance terms tonight so that you won't feel so intimidated, okay?"

Chrissy gave her a beaming smile. "Thanks, Cara," she said. "I'm glad I've got you around."

How easy it is to understand Chrissy, Caroline thought as they walked on in silence. *You always know exactly what she's thinking. When she's down, she's really down, and when she's excited, the whole world has to know about it! She's like*

Peter Pan compared to all the other kids at school. We all think we're being cool, but sometimes I wonder if we haven't turned into boring, middle-aged people already!

Suddenly Chrissy froze and gazed up at the sky. "Look!" she whispered. Caroline looked up obediently, but couldn't see anything unusual. She glanced back at Chrissy, who was staring into the sky, lost in wonder. Caroline shifted nervously from one foot to the next, then looked back hopefully at the sky again. She began to wonder if Chrissy was experiencing some kind of supernatural vision, then decided that her cousin wasn't the sort to have visions like that. She was too down-to-earth.

"What are you looking at?" Caroline asked at last.

"The geese," Chrissy answered. "See the wild geese flying south?"

Caroline followed Chrissy's pointed finger and saw a faint V shape in the evening haze. "Oh, yes, geese," she said politely, wondering if Chrissy considered them an omen or something.

"They're the first geese I've seen here," Chrissy said, still standing as if in a trance.

"You saw some in the lake at Golden Gate Park," Caroline reminded her.

"I mean wild geese."

"They were pretty wild in the park," Caroline joked. "Don't you remember how that one tried to peck your leg?"

Chrissy didn't even smile. "You don't understand," she said in a tight voice. "The wild geese are one of the big signs of fall at home. Sometimes you can hear them all night, calling to each other as they pass overhead. When we see them we know that winter is on the way, and we hurry up with all the outside chores. The moment my mom hears the first geese passing over, she always yells, 'Henry, time to get on the storm windows!' So Dad puts on all the storm windows and we check the locks on the barn doors, and the roof tiles and the hay. Mom counts all the jars in the cellar to make sure we have enough in case of emergencies, and sticks up the draft tape around the windows. Seeing the geese made me realize that we don't even know what season of the year it is here."

"Sure we do," Caroline said, pausing by a big maple tree in the sidewalk. "The trees turn red and yellow here the same as everywhere else."

"Correction," Chrissy said, eyeing the red maple leaves critically. "The *tree* turns red, in the singular. This is the only tree I've seen that's changed color in this whole city."

"Chrissy, that is just not true. We have lots of trees in the city," Caroline protested.

"Yes, but most of them are evergreens. They're either eucalyptus or pine trees and they don't change color. You should see the trees at home, Cara. Whole big banks of red and gold around each house, and yellow willow leaves fluttering everywhere along the creek, and great piles of leaves to run through. . . ." She paused and patted the tree, as if it were a large animal. "This poor old thing here is the only one who's putting on a fall show for us. Otherwise we wouldn't even know. It's like living in a plastic bubble. . . ."

"At least you won't have to shovel snow here," Caroline said gently.

Chrissy looked up and laughed. "You're right about that," she said, nodding. "I should be counting my blessings! I guess fall always makes me feel sad, and this year whenever I feel sad, I think of home. I can imagine the trees around our house all red and gold, and the big roaring fire, and the smell of baking, and everything seems so far away."

"You're still planning to go home for Christmas, aren't you?" Caroline asked. "That's not too far away now. Of course, I realize that having to put up with me for another couple of months without a break is not too wonderful—"

Chrissy grabbed her arm. "Having you for an adopted sister is pretty neat," she said. "In fact that's the best thing about living here—getting to find out what it's like to have a sister. And you know what? I really like it. In fact I'd insist Mom and Dad had another baby, except I'd be in college and gone before a new sister was old enough to talk to me."

Caroline noticed that Chrissy had picked up her stride again and was bouncing down the sidewalk, just like her usual self. Amazing, Caroline thought, smiling fondly at her cousin. *There is nothing that can keep her down for long.*

Chapter 3

"Let's run through it again," Caroline said patiently, pushing her hair back from her eyes.

"Okay," Chrissy said. "I think I've got it now."

Caroline sat up Indian style on her bed, tucking her legs in under her as she watched Chrissy. "Now," she said, "first show me a jeté."

"Jeté," Chrissy said. "Yes, I think I remember that one. It's like this, right?" She spun around, sweeping the sheets of Caroline's English paper off the dresser.

"Chrissy!" Caroline interrupted her progress. Chrissy stopped in mid turn and looked back with a hurt look.

"Not that one?" she asked.

"That's a chaîné turn," Caroline said patiently, "and that's my English paper on the floor." She

reached her hand off the bed to retrieve the
paper. "A jeté is when you jump from foot to foot
with your knees up high."

"Oh, I remember now," Chrissy said, beaming
at Caroline. "You mean this one, right?" Chrissy
asked, and Caroline pulled her hand away as her
cousin began jumping in the air and pouncing on
the English paper before getting her foot tangled
up with the lamp cord. The lamp teetered for a
second on the edge of the dresser.

"Chrissy!" Caroline yelled, leaping up to make
an unsuccessful grab at the lamp as it crashed to
the floor.

"Holy mazoley!" Chrissy muttered, turning
around to look at the broken pieces of light bulb
lying over the rumpled sheets of paper. "Did I do
all that in one leap?"

"Yes, and it was the wrong leap," Caroline said
dryly, dropping to the floor to pick up the pieces
of glass with careful fingers. At least the bulb had
split into a few large fragments instead of shatter-
ing into tiny pieces. "I said jeté and you did pas
de chat."

"Pas de chat? What's that?" Chrissy asked
cautiously. "I don't remember that one at all."
She knelt beside Caroline and helped pick up the
glass.

"You know, I told you it was step of the cat. You
bring up one leg and the other one comes to join
it, and you put them both down again."

A smile flickered across Chrissy's face. "And
they call that step of the cat?" she asked.

Caroline nodded.

"Have you ever seen a cat doing that?" Chrissy asked.

Caroline had to smile. "It's supposed to be very light on the feet, like a cat," she said. "Although the way you did it just now. . ."

Chrissy grinned. "It was more like step of the dinosaur, right?"

"Pretty much," Caroline agreed.

Chrissy sank back on her heels. "Let's face it, Cara. I'm a hopeless case. I might just as well forget about these tryouts."

"You're not hopeless, Chrissy," Caroline said, carefully dropping the glass pieces into her wastebasket. "You move well. You just don't know ballet. And you don't dance too well in a small crowded bedroom."

"I know the sort of jazz dance cheerleaders do, and that's all." Chrissy admitted. "And there's no way I can pick up ballet in just one night. I can see that now. I thought it would just be a couple of names I'd have to learn, but there must be millions."

"I really think you're worrying for nothing," Caroline said kindly. "I bet a lot of those other girls haven't studied ballet either. They're just watching the teacher and picking up what she does. I know you could do that, too. After all, they don't want perfection—you're not trying out for the Bolshoi Ballet, you know."

Chrissy got up and turned away. "It's okay. I think I'll just forget about it. I bet there are lots of other things I could be doing after school. I could start taking healthy walks. . . . I could read more, broaden my mind while I'm here. . . ."

"But you were so excited about the play," Caroline reminded her. "It's *Oklahoma!*—about farms—you really wanted to be in it."

"I know," Chrissy said softly. She opened her top drawer and took out her nightshirt, still not looking at Caroline. "But I guess I'm not willing to look like a fool."

"What's gotten into you, Chrissy?" Caroline asked. "When you first got here, you were so spunky. You were ready to try anything once. And you didn't even mind laughing at yourself either. Look at that time you got knocked over by the wave. You were the first person to laugh then, and everyone thought you were terrific."

"I know," Chrissy said again, "I wasn't afraid to try anything when I first came here, because back home I'd always been able to do most things. Kids looked up to me at school. I was one of the hotshot cheerleaders. I was even one of the best dancers at Danbury High." Chrissy sighed. "Now I've been here long enough to know that I'm not too great at anything. I guess what I'm trying to say is that I've lost my confidence. I've come to a place where everybody does something well, and I know I can't compete. Let's face it, Cara, I'm just an ordinary girl. In fact, I'm more than ordinary, I'm mediocre!"

Caroline put her hand gently on Chrissy's

shoulder. "Don't say that, because it's not true," she said. "You're bursting with lots of talents. All you need is the training." Caroline paused, searching for the right words to make Chrissy feel better. She knew from years of experience how awful it was to lose your confidence. "If we went back to your school and I wanted to try out for cheerleader, you'd be much better than me, because you know the right kinds of moves. I'd probably learn quickly, because I know ballet, but it would take me a while to pick up the routines. It's just the same with you here: You know how to dance, you just have to pick up the routines."

"I used to think I was a pretty cool dancer," Chrissy said hesitantly, "but I'd never get a chance to show what I could do if I couldn't learn the tryout routine."

"Chrissy?" Caroline asked after a brief silence. "Would you like me to come to tryouts with you? I don't have my ballet class until five-thirty tomorrow."

Chrissy turned around slowly. "Would you do that?"

"If you want me to," Caroline said. "I could help you learn the routine. . . ."

Chrissy's face broke into a dazzling smile. "Caroline, you are the greatest person who ever existed," she said, flinging her arms around her cousin. "I'd definitely try out if you were there."

"Okay, okay, I'll come then," Caroline panted. "Now will you stop crushing me!"

The next afternoon both girls stood at the back of the auditorium, taking in the bustle and confusion going on around the stage. Two hefty boys were staggering across the floor with a spotlight. Several girls were doing stretches. A couple of people were singing a rowdy, foot-stomping song, while someone else was playing a ballad on the piano. Caroline had lent Chrissy her bright pink leotards and braided her hair into a long French braid in the girls locker room. She glanced at Chrissy, standing wide-eyed and tense beside her, and noted with satisfaction that Chrissy looked just right.

"Come on, let's go join the others," Caroline said brightly.

Chrissy grabbed her arm. "Let's just wait a while here first," she whispered.

"There's nothing to be nervous about," Caroline comforted. "Everyone here is in the same boat. They're all students here at Maxwell, just like you. Look, don't you recognize Melanie from your math class?"

"I know," Chrissy said, "but they all look so different today. They look like they know what they are doing."

"You'll be fine," Caroline said. "Come on. . ." She took Chrissy's arm and propelled her forward. As they approached the group of girls, she felt her own stomach tie itself into a tight knot. *You're as bad as Chrissy,* she scolded herself. *I don't know why you should be feeling nervous. You've been to enough real auditions in your life—this is just kid's stuff, and what's more, you're only here as a coach. You're not even trying out!*

But even the internal pep talk could not untie the knot in her stomach. *It's just the thought of facing all these people I hardly know,* she decided. *I hope I outgrow this dumb shyness one day. I thought being with Chrissy might help me, but all I've done is make Chrissy as shy and tense as I am.*

Caroline swallowed hard, put on her brightest smile, and steered Chrissy into the middle of the group. One or two of the girls looked up and smiled at Caroline as she joined them.

"Aren't you the one who does ballet?" one of them asked. She was a tall redhead with lots of freckles, and Caroline recognized her as a cheerleader. "I didn't realize I was going to have to compete with professionals," she went on. But she said it as a joke, and Caroline instantly felt better. She rolled the word "professional" around inside her head, liking the way it sounded.

"I'm not really trying out," she whispered back to the girl. "I'm just here with my cousin—to give her moral support."

"I'm Jan, by the way," the girl said. She smiled across at Chrissy. "Are you a ballerina, too?" she asked. "You sure look like one."

"Not me," Chrissy said. "I don't know a step of the cat from a step of the ox!"

The girl giggled. "Me neither," she said, "but I fake it."

Just then a loud voice called, "All those students trying out for the dancing chorus get on
stage."

"That's Miss Barker, one of the P.E. teachers,"
Caroline whispered to Chrissy. "Is she the one
who was calling out the ballet steps yesterday?"

Chrissy nodded. Caroline looked at Miss Barker
skeptically. "I don't think she knows her step of
the cat from the step of the ox either," she
muttered to Chrissy under her breath, "so you've
got nothing to worry about!"

She gave Chrissy a friendly push. "Go on, up
on stage."

Chrissy shot her a look of horror. "Aren't you
coming, too?"

"I'll stand in the wings and whisper instructions
if you need them," Caroline said reassuringly.
"But don't worry, you're going to be great."

Chrissy grabbed at Caroline's sleeve. "Come up
and dance with me, please," she said. "I need you
standing right beside me, so I don't turn the
wrong way. You saw how I knocked over the
lamp—I'd never get picked if I did that to the
teacher!"

"But I'm not dressed right," Caroline said, looking down at her black cords and big blue sweater,
and knowing it was a lame excuse.

"Please, Cara," Chrissy begged. "I really need
you!"

"All right people, listen up now," Miss Barker
yelled.

"You can see why she's called Barker, can't

you?" Caroline whispered to Chrissy. Chrissy hardly smiled. Her eyes were still on Caroline, pleading with her to come on stage.

"I want all those students who did not learn the routine yesterday up here first," Miss Barker went on. "Two lines please. Girls at the front. Boys at the back."

About eight girls walked hesitantly onto the stage. Two boys shuffled into the line behind them, looking around as if preparing an escape route. Chrissy hesitated, then dragged Caroline with her.

"Chrissy!" Caroline hissed crossly, but Chrissy just looked at her with soulful eyes. *I hate when she makes that sad little puppy dog face,* Caroline thought. *But I may as well make sure that she gets picked.*

"Now let's pay attention so that I only have to show you this once," Miss Barker instructed in her drill-sergeant voice. "It goes like this: step close, step close, pas de bourre, chaîné, chaîné. Then back in the other direction. Got it? That's the opening sequence. We'll get that right first."

Chrissy shot Caroline a frightened look. "Easy," Caroline whispered. "Just watch my feet. You can do all those things."

"Now try it," Miss Barker ordered. The dancers stumbled their way across the stage, bumping into each other as they turned at different moments.

"And again," Miss Barker sighed. "Pick up your feet. You are not marching, you are dancing."

"Do it once more for me, Cara," Chrissy whispered. "I can't get that middle bit right."

Caroline moved through it rapidly.

"You, in the blue sweater—what's your name?" Miss Barker commanded.

"Caroline Kirby," Caroline mumbled, "but you see I'm only here to—"

Miss Barker obviously wasn't interested in explanations. "Come out here for a minute," she commanded. "Now, all you people, and my chorus people from yesterday, too. I want you to watch how Caroline does it—go again, please."

Her face crimson with embarrassment, Caroline danced the routine. The steps were easy for her, but she had to concentrate very hard, conscious of all those eyes watching her.

"Very nice, dear," Miss Barker said when she had finished. "Did you all notice how she used her arms? She didn't just let them hang by her sides like wet noodles. She didn't stick them out like tree limbs, she moved them. Now, I want you all to try that."

Gradually they added more steps to the routine, then they went through it again and again, and finally they put it to music. Caroline's cheeks were still hot, and she was aware of the rest of the group sneaking looks at her and copying her movements.

"You're doing just great," Caroline whispered to Chrissy as they paused for a rest. "I don't think you need me here at all. You've learned the routine as quickly as any of them."

"Only because I had you right beside me to watch," Chrissy said. She turned and gave Caroline a huge grin. "But aren't you glad I got you to come? Thanks to me, you're an instant celebrity."

"Thanks for nothing," Caroline muttered back. "Now everyone is watching me, and you know how I hate that!"

"You are funny," Chrissy said with a grin. "If that was me that got to dance for everyone, I'd be as proud as anything. I don't understand you. How come you don't mind performing in a ballet?"

"That's different. When I'm all made up and in costume, I don't seem to mind it," Caroline replied. "It's as if it's not really me. Besides, when I'm on stage, the house lights are out and I can't see faces too clearly."

"Okay, listen up," Miss Barker commanded. "We'll run through it now with the people who were here yesterday, then we'll make our selections. We need six girls and six boys for the dancing chorus, but anyone who isn't chosen can join in with our singers."

"I wish I was a boy," Chrissy remarked as more and more students filed up to crowd the stage. "There are only six of them trying out. Look how many girls there are!"

"You'll do fine," Caroline encouraged. "Just dance. Don't think about impressing anyone or about the steps. Just dance. That's what I always do."

The music started. Legs and arms moved to-

gether. Caroline felt a surge of excitement as she
moved with the group. It was always exciting to
dance in a chorus—to feel that she was a small
but important part of the whole, one limb of a
giant creature, not an individual person at all.
She was almost sorry when Miss Barker clapped
her hands and the music stopped.

"Very nice," Miss Barker was saying. She
walked down to confer with two shadowy figures
sitting at the back of the hall. Most of the kids on
stage whispered and giggled nervously, while a
few calmly stretched or sat with their legs hanging over the edge of the stage. Chrissy, as usual
when she was nervous, talked nonstop until Miss
Barker came back to the stage.

"These are the people we've selected," she
said. "If you are not called, go over to Laura with
the clipboard and sign up for the singing chorus."
She walked out onto the stage. "First, since we
only have six boys, we're going to need all of
you!" she said. Everyone laughed and the boys
all blushed as the girls turned to look at them.
"Also, we'd like the young lady with the red hair,
you in the black leotard, Nancy Chin, the girl on
the end down there, Caroline, and the blond girl
beside you. Would you all stand together so that
we can judge you for height."

Those chosen shuffled toward the front of the
stage, looking embarrassed and pleased at the
same time. Chrissy gave Caroline a delighted
hug, then turned to congratulate Jan. Caroline
stood on the stage, absorbing the scene around

her, then she jumped down and ran forward to touch Miss Barker's arm. "Look, Miss Barker, I wasn't really trying out," she said. "I only came along to help out my cousin."

Miss Barker looked as if she couldn't believe what she was hearing. "But you were the best one here," she said. "We really need you. It was hard picking the others because they were all pretty much the same, but you were outstanding."

"That's because I study ballet," Caroline said. "That takes up all of my time." She was pleased by Miss Barker's compliments, but there was no way she could fit play rehearsals in between ballet lessons and everything else.

"But we really need you," Miss Barker pleaded. Caroline was conscious of the silence behind her, of people watching her and listening to her conversation. Was she sounding like a stuck-up brat?

"I was hoping you'd help coach the others," Miss Barker said. "We could use a dance expert to help out with the play."

"It's just a question of time," Caroline said hesitantly. She didn't want the kids listening to think she was too good for a little school play.

"Our rehearsal schedule shouldn't be very demanding for the chorus," Miss Barker said. "And I'm sure we could accommodate your other dance schedule."

"I don't know what to say," Caroline replied. Part of her was flattered that Miss Barker wanted her to be in the play so badly, while another part was reminding her that her present ballet classes left precious little time for homework and sleeping.

"Why don't we try it for a couple of weeks," Miss Barker suggested. "Then if it's really too much for you, we'll get someone else to take your place. I'm going to choose a couple of understudies from among the singers, just in case, so you wouldn't have to feel bad about dropping out."

"Okay, I guess I'll try it," Caroline said at last.

"Good for you," Miss Barker said heartily. "Now listen up, everyone. Line up and give me your names and phone numbers so that we know where to contact you."

What have I done? Caroline asked herself as she stood in line beside Chrissy. *I've already got one dance teacher who acts like a drill sergeant. Now it looks as though I've just got myself another!*

Chapter 4

"So aren't you glad I made you come along to tryouts with me?" Chrissy asked Caroline as they walked home from rehearsal the following Monday. The sun was glowing golden in their faces as it sank over the ocean, and the warmth of the unusually hot October day was still rising from the sidewalk.

"I guess so," Caroline said, unwilling to admit what she was really feeling. After all, how could she be so elated about dancing in a simple school musical when she hardly ever felt that way about ballet! But she had to admit to herself that she did feel elated. It seemed as if a great big happy bubble was growing inside her. Everything about the musical was fun. The people were fun, the play was fun, and even the director was fun.

"So how do you like Greg?" Chrissy asked, kicking at some dry leaves so that they crunched in a satisfying way. "Isn't he a total babe?"

Caroline nodded. "He's very nice," she said, grinning. What an understatement! Caroline had shown up for the first rehearsal prepared for a rigorous workout with Miss Barker. Instead she had found a slim young man in jeans and torn T-shirt sitting at the edge of the stage, eating a Big Mac. He had jumped up with the agility of a cat when the dancers entered the auditorium, and announced that he was the director.

"Where's Miss Barker?" Caroline had stammered, taking in the mass of dark curls, the dark, sensitive-looking eyes, and the fine bones of his face.

His serious look vanished and his whole face lit up as he gave her a broad grin. "Would you rather have her as director?" he asked. "I can leave if I'm not wanted."

Everyone had giggled, and he'd introduced himself as a drama major from San Francisco State who was directing the play for a class project. Miss Barker and a couple of other teachers would be supervising, but the real direction would be his.

Having Greg as the director changed everything in Caroline's eyes. He knew what he wanted on stage, and his ideas for routines were very good without being complicated. Caroline loved being able to do everything easily, and she basked in Greg's constant praise. Best of all, he believed that rehearsals should be fun, so he hardly ever yelled.

"He's certainly an improvement on Miss Barker, isn't he?" Chrissy asked. "I love all those exercises, and especially the back rubs." She paused and grinned at Caroline. "I'm just dying for Greg to give me a back rub!"

Caroline smiled and didn't say anything. She had surprised herself by loving the exercises and back rubs as much as Chrissy. Until recently she'd felt uneasy when anyone hugged her, or even got too close to her—except Alex, of course. But Greg had made his cast do all sorts of things, like massaging each other's feet, or pretending that they were mirror images of each other with their hands pressed tightly together. At first Caroline had been embarrassed, but one day Greg had chosen her for his partner to demonstrate a drill, and she'd actually felt the energy flowing from his palms into hers.

"So do you think I'm doing okay?" Chrissy asked. "You do it all so well that the rest of us get inferiority complexes."

"You're doing great," Caroline answered.

She'd said this without thinking, but now, as she visualized Chrissy dancing, she realized how much Chrissy had improved since the audition. She had so much energy when she danced, and threw herself into each routine with enthusiasm. Caroline felt proud of Chrissy, as if she were personally responsible for her cousin doing so well. *I did teach her enough to get chosen, didn't*

I? she asked herself. *I'm so glad she got picked—she's having such a great time. It would have been awful if I'd gotten picked and Chrissy hadn't.*

"Chrissy," she said hesitantly. "I don't always say what I feel, but I just wanted to tell you that I'm glad we're doing this together. I don't remember having this much fun before."

"Me, too," Chrissy said, beaming at Caroline. "This is without a doubt the best thing that's happened to me since I came to San Francisco."

"Even better than Hunter?" Caroline teased.

"Definitely better than Hunter," Chrissy said firmly. "All the time I was with Hunter, I felt as if I were acting a part. Now I really am acting a part, but I feel I can relax and be myself. Isn't that odd?"

"Not really," Caroline said. "I feel the same way. It's the atmosphere that Greg has created. He doesn't want us to feel uptight, so we're not."

"I can't wait to start rehearsing with the singers and actors next week," Chrissy said excitedly. "Who is this Sean Whatsit who's playing the lead?"

"I don't know him, but I've seen him around," Caroline answered. "He's a senior."

"Is he cute?"

"I guess so."

"Very cute?"

"I guess so."

"Super cute?"

Caroline laughed. "Chrissy, don't you think of anything else except boys?"

"Sure I do, sometimes," Chrissy said. "But having a boyfriend a thousand miles away is not the easiest thing in the world. Of course, I plan to stay faithful to Ben—especially after the Hunter fiasco—but that doesn't stop me from looking, does it?"

"Of course not," Caroline said. "As long as you don't ask me to give you sophistication lessons, like with Hunter, and as long as you don't look at Alex either!"

"I don't have much chance to look at Alex," Chrissy said thoughtfully. "You two hardly ever see each other these days."

"We went to a movie last Saturday," Caroline said defensively.

Chrissy didn't answer, and they walked on in silence to the top of the hill.

Caroline looked at her watch. "I think I'd better go right to ballet class," she said. "I haven't really got time to eat."

"But you need to eat," Chrissy insisted. "You can't go from lunchtime to late evening with no food. Remember how you almost fainted when you tried to diet too much? I don't want that to happen to you again."

"Don't worry, I won't try to do anything dumb like that again," Caroline said. "I'll pick up some macaroni salad as I pass the deli, okay?"

"Okay. But make sure that you get a drink with it," Chrissy said. "You need to replace lost liquids after all that leaping around."

"Yes, Mommy," Caroline said sweetly.

Chrissy giggled. "Well, someone has to take care of you. With a schedule like yours it's all too easy to skip meals. Luckily I don't have your problem. I'd skip practically anything before I skipped dinner."

"I'd better be going," Caroline said. "I don't want to be late for class again. Madame was mad enough on Friday after I stayed behind, talking to Greg. See ya, Chrissy. Tell Mom where I am." Then she turned and waved before setting off down the other side of the hill.

She was just coming out of the deli with her salad when she bumped into Tracy Wong, one of her best friends.

"Talk about great minds thinking alike!" Tracy said with a delighted smile. "You couldn't get home without a secret snack either?"

"Oh, I'm not on my way home," Caroline said. "Unfortunately I have to face two hours of ballet, and I couldn't go straight from rehearsal to that with no food."

"I should think not," Tracy said. "And you're only getting a salad, too. I was thinking of some chocolate cheesecake. Sure you won't join me in a piece—my treat?"

"I'd better not," Caroline said hesitantly. "I don't want to put on weight."

Tracy laughed. "You?" she asked. "With all the exercise you get, you could eat the entire deli counter before you started having problems. Why, I bet you guys burned up a whole slice of cheesecake during rehearsal this afternoon."

"Were you spying on us?" Caroline asked, falling into line with Tracy again.

"I was next door singing," Tracy said grandly. "Didn't you hear my lovely voice floating through the partition?"

"I heard some strange noises," Caroline said jokingly. "Is that what it was—you singing?"

"Hey, watch it," Tracy said. "You're talking to a member of the vocal chorus of *Oklahoma!*"

"But Tracy," Caroline said. "I've heard you sing before. You sounded like the foghorn out in the bay."

"So I've improved since then," Tracy said with a grin. "In fact I'll have you know that I am not half bad when I sing—at least I'm good enough for the chorus, when my voice can be disguised by all the others."

"I'm glad you're in the play," Caroline said. "It's a lot of fun, isn't it? Is Greg directing you guys as well?"

A big smile spread over Tracy's face. "Why do you think I joined the chorus?" she asked. "I'm not dumb, you know. When I heard that the chorus was short of singers and that the director was tall, dark, and handsome, that was enough for me."

"So we'll be rehearsing together soon," Caroline said. "That will be fun. I really like rehearsals so far. There's a good feeling about this production—everyone's so relaxed, and nobody ever yells, and it doesn't even matter too much if you come in on the wrong foot."

"Or the wrong note," Tracy added. "I wish this line would hurry up before I die of starvation. That woman is taking ages. How can anyone eat that much salami?"

Suddenly Caroline heard a clock chiming in the distance. She glanced down at her watch. "Oh, help," she said. "Look, Tracy, I can't hang around any longer or I'll be late for class. I'll take a rain check on the cheesecake—I've got to run. See ya!" and she pushed her way out of the deli, sprinting down the hill with long strides.

She was panting as she let herself into the back door of the ballet school. It was in an old brick building, only a couple of blocks from Union Square and behind an expensive department store, but it wasn't at all glamorous to look at. The entrance was in an alleyway that always smelled of garbage and old orange peel, and the iron staircase leading to the door of the school was more like a fire escape. Today Caroline took the steps two at a time. The changing room was empty, and Caroline felt as if she were competing for the world's record in quick changing as she ripped off her jeans and wriggled into her practice clothes. As usual when she was in a hurry, her head got stuck in the neck of her sweater and her tights refused to reveal where the leg openings were. Finally, feeling sweaty and tense, Caroline ran through into the practice room.

As she opened the door she was relieved to see that class hadn't actually started. The students were lounging around on the barres while Madame paced up and down talking to them.

"So you can appreciate zee importance of zis," she was saying in her strong French accent. "It will be a grand chance for any of you zat I feel is ready. I will not recommend all of you, please understand zat. Only my very best pupils—zee ones I am most proud of will go to zee test."

"What's she talking about?" Caroline asked as she crept to her place beside her friend Tais at the barre.

"A dance competition," Tais whispered back. "Next month. They're giving summer scholarships to a couple of major ballet companies."

"Wow," Caroline said softly. "Did she say who'll be going yet?"

"Only a few of us," Tais mouthed, not taking her eyes off Madame, who was staring in their direction.

"So young ladies and men," Madame went on grandly, "if I choose to teach you a new routine to dance for zis contest, I want your commitment—one hundred and ten percent of your commitment. Is zat clear? It will be a case of practice, practice, and more practice to achieve perfection! No other interests, no ball games or parties or any other excuses. Now, let us begin our warm-ups. Fifth position, port de bras with plié, begin!"

The music began. Caroline went mechanically through the familiar exercises, her hand reaching above her head then bending to sweep the floor, coming to rest then pivoting to change sides. *I*

don't know why I'm so worried, she thought.
*After all, Madame will not be likely to choose me.
I'm certainly not ready for a professional company.*

The class went on. Madame seemed determined to make all of them into perfect ballerinas overnight. "Leap higher, higher," she would scream. "I want you to hang in zee air, like a dandelion clock. Light as a feather!"

Caroline's turn came. She ran, leaped, and leaped again.

"I said like a dandelion, Caroline," Madame's voice boomed. "Not a three-hundred-pound lion. Go and do it again! You did not hang for one second."

Caroline wiped the sweat from her face and walked back slowly to the starting position. Her whole body felt exhausted. A quick mental calculation revealed that she had already spent nearly three hours dancing that afternoon, but she didn't want to perform poorly in front of her classmates. She made a supreme effort and flung herself into the leap.

"Better," Madame said crisply. "Put more effort into your work, Caroline. Remember what I said about one hundred and ten percent effort. Zat's what it will mean to have a chance at zee scholarship."

Caroline ran to the back of the line breathing heavily and with a funny feeling in her stomach. Had Madame just hinted that she was one of the people being considered for the scholarship contest? She fought back the urge to yell out in the middle of class, "Not me. I don't want it!" Instead she kept on dancing, forcing her tired limbs to move with everyone else's.

I'll tell her after the class, Caroline promised herself. *I'll tell her that I don't want to be considered.*

After the last exercise she pulled on her sweater and went straight up to Madame.

"Ah, Caroline, my dear," Madame said before Caroline could open her mouth to speak. "There is much zat I have wanted to say to you. I am glad zat you come to me."

"Yes, Madame," Caroline said. "You see, it's this scholarship—"

"Of course it is," Madame cut it. "You worry if you are good enough, if you will be chosen—but I say to you: Caroline, you have zee talent. You are one of my students I have zee great hopes for. You could be zee one to go to zee ballet in New York, but only if you are prepared to make zee big sacrifices!"

"But Madame," Caroline began, and again Madame cut her short.

"No excuses. I want to hear no excuses. I see zat your heart and soul are not in your work all zee time. Zis must change, Caroline. You must make zee effort. Twice last week you come in late, and when you come you dance like zis . . . like zee potatoes, no energy. I want to see you float zee way I know you can float. Work, Caroline, zat is what I require from you—work and more work! Now please leave me. I am tired."

With that Madame swept away, leaving Caroline feeling angry and confused, with only her reflection staring back at her from the mirrored walls to console her.

Chapter 5

Later that night Caroline hesitated outside the open door of her parents' bedroom. She could see her mother sitting at the vanity table, brushing her long hair, still naturally dark and luxurious, without a touch of gray. As Caroline gazed through the doorway, she thought that her mother should have been the ballet dancer instead of her. She'd often thought that. There was a smooth, elegant grace about everything her mother did, which Caroline knew she'd never have. Even simply brushing her hair, with no makeup on her face and wrapped in an old silk robe, her mother looked just right.

Edith Kirby caught sight of her daughter in the mirror. "Hello, honeybun, how's your busy schedule going? Are you still managing to juggle school, dancing, Alex, and the new play?" she asked with a smile as she counted off Caroline's interests on her fingers.

Caroline sighed and sat on the edge of the big, satin-quilted bed.

"That was a big sigh for such a little person," her mother said, swiveling around to face Caroline. "Does that mean that everything is getting to be too much for you?"

"I have a problem, Mom," Caroline said. "I've been playing around with it all the way home and I still don't know what to do."

Caroline's mother said nothing, but nodded and waited for her daughter to speak.

Caroline took a deep breath. "It's trying to juggle ballet and the play at school that's the problem," she said.

Her mother nodded again. "I thought you were taking on one thing too many when you agreed to dance in the musical," she said.

"I thought I could handle both of them," Caroline said, running her hand over the smooth surface of the satin as she spoke, "and I think I could have if Madame hadn't started putting on all this extra pressure."

"Are the school rehearsals making you too tired for your real practices?" Edith Kirby asked.

"I didn't think they were," Caroline said. "We don't exactly have to work out too hard in the school chorus, but there is a big ballet competition coming up, and the winners get scholarships for a summer session with a New York ballet.

Madame seems to think I have a chance—"

"Caroline, that's wonderful," her mother interrupted. "That must make you feel really good—to know that all your hard work is finally paying off."

"I guess so," Caroline said hesitantly.

"I must tell your father the moment he gets in," her mother went on excitedly, while Caroline continued to play with the satin bed cover. "He'll finally have to admit that I'm right!"

"About what?" Caroline asked, looking up to see her mother's face glowing with pleasure.

"About you, of course. I remember the first day I started you in ballet school, when you were six. I watched you dance and you seemed to be so much more talented than all the other little girls. I came rushing home to tell your father that we had given birth to a future star. Your father tried to bring me back down to earth again—you know how he is. He told me that just because you could skip around a room with your toes pointed did not necessarily mean that you were heading for the Bolshoi. But I knew, way back then. I said to him, 'You just wait until she's accepted by a major company and she's dancing *Swan Lake*, then you'll admit I was right.' "

"I'm not dancing *Swan Lake* yet, Mom," Caroline said uneasily. "I haven't even been officially chosen to represent the school in the competition."

"I'm sure you will be," her mother said, "if you put your mind to it and work extra hard. Dad and

I will help you in any way we can, of course."

"Thanks, Mom," Caroline said, "but don't expect too much, okay? I don't want you to blame me or anything if I don't get chosen."

"Of course we wouldn't blame you, honey," Caroline's mother said, her voice rising in a tone of dismay. "You can only do your best. Imagine, a summer in New York, dancing with the top ballerinas in the country. . . ." Her face took on a wistful look, as if it were she who would dance *Swan Lake*, and not Caroline.

Caroline swallowed hard. Somehow this conversation was not going the way she wanted. "But Madame says it will mean a lot of extra work," she said. "I don't know if I have time—"

"Of course you don't right now," her mother said. "You've taken on too many things as usual. This silly school musical—"

"What about the musical?" Caroline asked defensively.

"Don't you think it might be the wrong time to get involved with a school production?" her mother asked. "Maybe you'll have to let it go, this year."

"Give up the musical?" Caroline stammered. "But I like the musical. It's fun."

"I'm sure it is, honeybun, but you don't want it to stand in the way of your future, do you?" her mother asked. "Think about it, Caroline, if it's making you too tired to do your ballet properly, then it has to go, doesn't it? After all, dancing in school musicals is really for people who have no other place to perform. You might have all the stages in the world one day."

Down the hall a door slammed. Her mother leaped up. "I bet that's your father now. I can't wait to tell him the news. He'll be so excited. . . ." She rushed out before Caroline could say anything more.

For the rest of the week Caroline went around feeling as if she were carrying a huge weight on her shoulders. She went to school, where she did her work well; she went to musical rehearsal, where she danced the routines; and she went to ballet school, where Madame yelled at her as usual—but she did everything as if she were a robot.

I can't go on like this, that's for sure. she decided as she ran from one practice to another. *I feel as if I'm going to snap at any moment. Mom and Madame are both bugging me to give up the musical, but I don't want to do that. The problem is that I really like it. But if I do badly in the competition, they will never forgive me, and Mom and Dad have paid for ballet lessons all these years. They are right to expect some result at the end. . . . I wish I knew what to do.*

She tried talking to Chrissy about it as they walked home together.

"My mother is pressuring me to give up the musical," she said, kicking savagely at the dried leaves on the sidewalk. "Do you really think I should?"

"Give up the musical?" Chrissy echoed, looking up at her cousin. "But you love the musical. You said it was the most fun thing you've ever done."

"I know," Caroline said. "But it's taking energy I need for my real dance studies."

"Talk to Greg about it," Chrissy suggested. "He's very understanding. I'm sure he could give you a rehearsal schedule that fitted in with your other classes."

Caroline shrugged. "I don't know, Chrissy," she said. "It's not that the schedules clash, it's just that I'm so tired when I get to ballet, and my teacher notices that I'm not dancing at full speed."

"Do you really want this scholarship?" Chrissy asked bluntly.

Caroline kicked more leaves. "I guess so," she said. "After all, I've been training for ten years to get into a big ballet company, haven't I? It does seem kind of dumb to throw that all away just for a high school play."

"But you're the best one in the chorus, Caroline. The rest of us need you to help us with the steps. The whole dance chorus will fall to pieces if you drop out!"

"I'm sure it won't, Chrissy. After all, it's only easy little dances. Anyone could do it!"

"Oh, I get it," Chrissy said angrily. "You don't think the rest of us are good enough for you. You don't think a high school production is worth your time. Where's your school spirit?" She strode ahead so that Caroline had to run to keep up with her.

"I don't think that, Chrissy," Caroline protested. "I have a great time with you, and I love working with Greg . . . but you must admit, it's only high school. No scout from a New York ballet is going to come see it."

"I know one thing," Chrissy insisted. "Nothing would make me give up the one thing that was fun in my life. I would make time for it! But then I wasn't born dedicated like you!"

After that Caroline dropped the subject with Chrissy. Her cousin obviously thought she was a snob to put her ballet before the high school production. She tried talking to Alex, too, but he was no help either.

"If you want the scholarship, I suppose you have to go for it," he said hesitantly on Saturday night as they devoured a pepperoni pizza. "But I think you're too young to give up your entire life for ballet. What about us, Cara? I never see you anymore—you're either running to a rehearsal or from a rehearsal, or you're doing homework after a rehearsal. That's no way to live. You have to enjoy yourself when you're a teenager. You're already living an old person's life. You need some fun."

Sometimes Caroline felt that what he said made good sense. Then her mother would remind her that a major ballet company was what she'd been working toward all these years, and she knew that that made sense, too. She tried to keep on with the musical and with her ballet. She

tried extra hard at both the following week, so
that neither Greg nor Madame could accuse her
of not giving her best, but the strain left her
feeling tired and drained. At home she snapped
at Chrissy when Chrissy was too long in the
bathroom or sang in the kitchen. At school her
teachers accused her of daydreaming, and both
Greg and Madame did notice something was
wrong, in spite of her efforts.

"Caroline, you are so tense," Madame said to
her after class. "Look at your shoulders. You hold
them so, as if zey were made of steel. Zee judges,
zey do not want to watch zee steel person dance,
zey wish to watch zee graceful butterfly."

Greg also caught her after a rehearsal. "Hey,
Caroline, loosen up," he said, giving her shoulders
a friendly massage. "You're being too serious
about this. It's a fun play—we're being a bunch of
Okies dancing around a ranch, we're not the
chorus at the Bolshoi. You're trying to make
everything too perfect, and it's standing out. The
others can't do the sort of lifts you can. And your
face, Cara—you look as if you're doing punish-
ment duty." He pulled such a terrible face that
Caroline had to laugh.

"That's more like it," he said, giving her a
friendly pat on the back. "Just enjoy it, okay?"

Caroline longed to tell him the truth, to say,
"You see, I'm trying to please everybody at once
and be in two places at once, and it just isn't
working," but by the time she got up enough
courage to form the sentence inside her head,

Greg had run off to talk to another group about scenery.

Then, after a Friday rehearsal, everything sorted itself out. Greg asked all the dancers to stay for a report on their progress. He told them how pleased he was with all of them and how they were already beginning to dance like a real chorus line.

"I think it's about time we started to work on our solo numbers," he said. "I have a couple of small solos for the boys in the Kansas City number, and I'm going to put in a terrific solo for one of the girls at the hoedown. I had it in mind even before I started working with you, and as it happens, we have one young lady here who is just right for the part. I know she's going to dazzle us all with her fancy moves."

Caroline could feel her cheeks burning so she looked down at her feet.

"I know she's also going to tell me that she can't handle it . . ." Greg went on.

I'll make a way to handle it, Caroline thought. She could see herself, dressed in ginghams and lace petticoats, dancing while all the others clapped, showing what a *real* dancer could do.

". . . but I know she can handle it, if she just believes in herself. What do you say, Chrissy?"

Caroline looked up. Had she heard right? She glanced over at her cousin, then back at her feet. It was true.

"You mean you want me to do the solo?"

Chrissy stammered.

"Sure thing," Greg said, beaming at her. "You'll be great."

The group broke up and the others crowded around Chrissy to congratulate her.

"And you thought you wouldn't even be good enough to make the chorus," one of them was teasing. "Remember how scared you were?"

And she only made it because I helped her, Caroline thought bitterly. How could Greg give Chrissy the solo? She hardly knew one dance step from another. Greg himself had said that Caroline was the only real dancer in the group, and yet he'd given the solo to someone else. Where was the fairness in that?

At least it makes one thing easy, she decided. *I'm certainly not hanging around to watch Chrissy make a fool of herself. She'll probably beg me to help her with the steps. But at least I won't be here, where my energy would be wasted.*

She hurried after Greg. "I've been meaning to talk to you," she said. I'm afraid I've got to quit the chorus."

Greg's eyes narrowed for a second. "Is this because I gave the solo to Chrissy and not you?" he asked.

"Of course not," Caroline said, in what she hoped was a confident voice. "I've been trying to get up enough courage to tell you for days . . . you see, I have to work extra hard at my ballet now. I'm hoping to represent my ballet school in a big competition on the East Coast."

"Congratulations," Greg said.

"So you see," Caroline went on, "I really don't have time anymore, even for a chorus. I didn't want to be in it in the first place. I only came along with Chrissy to help boost her confidence. Now that she's doing just fine without me, I can go back to my proper ballet studies and let another girl take my place." The words tumbled out, faster and faster. When she had finished, Greg didn't say a thing, but just looked at her.

"I've got to go," she mumbled, her cheeks still burning with embarrassment and anger. As she turned to leave, Greg touched her arm gently. "We'll miss you, Cara," he said. "Good luck."

As Caroline hurried from the hall, a group around the piano started singing "I'm Just a Girl Who Can't Say No"—one of the songs from the play. Caroline looked back at them and noticed Chrissy right there in the middle of the group. They all had their arms draped around each other's shoulders, and laughed as they sang. Caroline watched for a moment, then with a heavy sigh ran out of the hall and into the cool autumn afternoon.

Chapter 6

It was dark when Caroline pushed open the front door and dropped her ballet bag in the hall. She could hear voices coming from her bedroom—or rather, the bedroom she shared with Chrissy. The high-pitched giggle had to be Tracy's. *So Tracy's over here again!* she thought angrily. *She and Chrissy have been spending an awful lot of time together since I quit the musical last week. Not only did Chrissy get my solo, but now she's taking over my friend!*

She walked down the hall toward her bedroom. Another burst of giggles dropped suddenly into whispers. Caroline pushed open the door and was surprised to find the room in darkness.

"What are you guys doing?" she asked, reaching out for the light switch. Suddenly she drew back her hand in horror—instead of the light switch, she'd touched something slimy and cold.

"What's going on—" she began, taking a step forward. Suddenly she let out a scream as something brushed against her face.

Someone turned on the light, and Chrissy and Tracy stood facing Caroline, both looking delighted. "You see, it works perfectly," Chrissy said.

Caroline looked from one laughing face to the next. "Is this your idea of a joke?" she stammered, still shaken by the slime and the cobweb, "because I don't find it very funny."

"We were just trying out some ideas for Halloween," Tracy said, trying to stifle her laughter and look concerned for Caroline. "The slime on the light switch was great, wasn't it?"

"Oh, great," Caroline said dryly. "A laugh a minute."

"And the cobwebs were my idea," Chrissy said brightly. "We did them at home once—you spread a little honey along cotton yarn."

Caroline looked at the black strands hanging from her ceiling and noticed, with relief, that she'd missed walking into a large rubber spider suspended nearby.

"Aren't you two a little old for this sort of thing?" she asked, walking across to her bed.

"We're trying out ideas for our Halloween party," Chrissy said.

"What Halloween party?"

"Tracy and I were both getting sentimental about Halloween," Chrissy went on excitedly. "We both used to love going out Trick or Treating, but Tracy thinks that we're too old for it now. I told her about the crazy parties we always used to have back home, so we decided to have a party here!"

She looked up at Caroline, but Caroline didn't make any comment.

"We thought we'd invite the whole cast of the play," Tracy went on, "but you know how small my apartment is. . . ."

"So I said I'd ask your folks if we could hold it here, and they thought it was a great idea!" Chrissy finished for her.

"I see," Caroline said. *Terrific, now she has parties at my house without asking me,* she thought, feeling the pressure building up inside her head. *I bet she asks all my friends. I wonder if I'm included.*

"We've been having the best time trying out these tricks," Tracy said, beaming at Caroline. "We've been laughing ourselves silly all evening!"

Caroline nodded, and swallowed back all the thoughts racing round inside her head.

"Chrissy has the neatest ideas," Tracy went on. "All the sorts of things I'd forgotten about that we used to do in grade school. Do you remember when we made a haunted house once and we peeled grapes for eyeballs and had cold spaghetti for guts? We're going to do stuff like that again."

"Don't you think we've outgrown grade-school stuff?" Caroline asked.

"Oh, come on, Cara, don't be such an old fuddy-duddy," Chrissy said. "You take life so seriously. It will be such fun—everyone needs to act crazy once in a while."

"As long as you don't expect me to peel grapes for you," Caroline said, pulling off her boots and flinging them into a corner, "because I don't have any time at all."

"How was your practice tonight?" Chrissy asked.

"Hard," Caroline said.

"I wish you hadn't had to drop out of the musical," Chrissy went on, "because it's great. You'd be so proud of me. I've learned all the steps for my little solo, and I haven't knocked over any chorus members yet."

"She's being modest, as usual," Tracy interrupted. "Our singing chorus rehearsed with the dancers today, and she's fantastic. You should see the way she can jump around in that number. Everybody was standing around, clapping to the music without being asked to, just watching her dance."

Chrissy laughed nervously. "Yeah, you'd better watch out, Caroline. I might turn out to be an undiscovered ballerina." She giggled. "And you'll be able to say you taught me the difference between the step of the cat and the step of the elephant!"

Caroline knew she was only joking, but she felt

a cold stab of fear, like a hand clutching at her heart. What if all that was true? What if Chrissy did turn out to be a better dancer, and all those years of practice were for nothing?

"Well, I bet you could be a ballerina if you wanted to," Tracy was saying to Chrissy. "I'm sure you'd be good enough if you studied hard like Cara."

Chrissy shook her head. "Not me," she said. "I haven't got Cara's dedication. Besides, I wouldn't want to go through all that stuff at ballet class. If her Madame yelled at me, I'd yell right back, and if she threw her banana at me, I'd throw it right back."

"Throw a banana?" Tracy asked.

Chrissy nodded. "When she gets mad at the students, she throws things. She threw her banana at Caroline one day and Caroline danced on top of it!"

Tracy hardly smiled. She looked at Caroline with concern. "You poor thing," she said. "I thought you hated being yelled at. Why don't you switch ballet schools?"

Caroline swallowed hard. She could feel a lump in the back of her throat that made it hard to talk. "She's the best teacher, I guess," she mumbled. Somehow, now that Chrissy and Tracy were both being nice to her, she felt guilty for being mad at them, but still couldn't get rid of her anger. *I guess I can't be a very nice person*, she thought.

"Well, I really admire you," Tracy went on.

"You're one of the few people I know who have a real ambition and are carrying it through. We'll all be so proud when you join a real ballet company and we see you on public TV."

"I've got a long way to go before that happens," Caroline said, trying to smile.

"No way—you're good enough already," Chrissy insisted. "You were really great when we saw you dance at your last performance. In fact, to be honest, I'm glad you quit the musical, because you showed the rest of us up."

Then how come I didn't get the solo? Caroline wanted to say, but didn't. Instead she pulled off her sweater and turned to leave the room. "I think I'll go get some food," she said. "I haven't eaten since lunch, and I have homework to get started on."

"We won't disturb you any longer," Tracy said, looking pointedly at Chrissy. "Why don't we go over to my place and start making invitations for the party."

"That's right—we'll leave you in peace, Cara," Chrissy said, and they tiptoed out as if she were an invalid or a little child.

The next night Caroline was home alone, just starting on her math homework, when Alex showed up.

"I know I don't have an appointment," he said, smiling, "but I'm not staying long. I just happened to be walking back from the library and I thought—I wonder if Caroline will allow me to stop by without an appointment?"

"You dope," Caroline said, laughing. "Come on in. I was dying for an excuse not to start my trig."

"So that's all I am to you, huh?" His face was semiserious. "Well, at least it seems that I still have one function in your life—I'm a good excuse!"

"Oh, Alex," Caroline said, reaching up to stroke his cheek. "If you knew how often I wished you were around. If only there were more time in the world."

"I remember when life used to be fun," Alex said, sitting on the sofa and pulling her down beside him. "Remember when we used to go on dates? When we danced and went to parties? Just what happened to life?"

"I wish I knew," Caroline said. "I'm longing to have fun again. I just wish I knew what fun was. Tracy and Chrissy are planning this big Halloween party. They say it's going to be the party of the year, but I don't even know that I want to go."

"Why not?" Alex asked in surprise.

"It's in my house," Caroline said nervously, "so I can hardly not go, can I?"

"But Cara, it will do you good—you need some fun," Alex said.

"You think it will be fun touching peeled grapes and pretending they're eyeballs?" Caroline asked. "The whole thing seems so juvenile, Alex."

"I think it will be fun!" Alex replied. "Is everybody going to come in costume? You liked wearing a costume for the masked ball, didn't you?

What do you think of me as Count Dracula?" He leaned over toward her, pinning her to the sofa and making a leering face. "I vant to suck your blood, blah, blah!"

Caroline pushed him gently away. "Cut it out, Alex," she said.

"What's wrong with you?" he asked, sitting up and looking offended. "Have you totally lost your sense of humor? I used to think you were a fun person."

"I guess I'm just too tired," Caroline said. "I'm always too tired these days."

"You sound like a commercial for iron-poor blood," Alex said, still attempting to joke.

"I wish I could solve my tiredness as easily as that," Caroline replied. "I get a good night's sleep, but I wake up just as tired the next morning."

"Maybe it's more stress than tiredness," Alex suggested.

"I know it is," Caroline said. "I feel pulled in ten different directions at once. I've got to do well in this contest, I've got to cope with watching Chrissy do the solo in the musical and becoming best friends with my best friend and inviting people to my house for a party—"

Alex put a hand on her arm to interrupt her. "Hey, if Chrissy's bugging you, why don't you talk to her about it?"

"What can I say, Alex?" Caroline asked hopelessly. "I can't tell her to stop seeing Tracy or stop being successful or even stop having a good time, because I don't want her to stop. Part of me is really glad for all the good things that are happening to her. It's just jealously, I suppose. I'm feeling all eaten up inside that she can enjoy life and I can't."

"You could if you decided to," Alex said. "You have to stop putting so much pressure on yourself."

"How can I?" Caroline asked miserably. "My whole future is at stake here. I've reached the stage when I find out if I can really be a professional dancer or not. My teacher and my parents expect so much of me, and I'm not sure I'm ready—I'm not sure if I'll ever be ready. That's what's making me so tense."

Alex squeezed her arm gently. "Have you ever stopped to ask yourself what you really want for *you*?" he asked gently. "Do *you* really want all this pressure?"

"Of course not," Caroline snapped. "Who would want to live feeling that their head is about to explode every day?"

"Then don't live like it," Alex said. "Decide what you really want. If you don't want to enter this competition, then don't."

"You don't know what you're talking about," Caroline said, wriggling clear of him and getting to her feet. "I have to enter it and what's more, I have to win it."

"Says who?" Alex demanded. "Other people or you?"

"Everybody," Caroline shouted. "Everybody, including me."

"I don't," Alex said quietly. "I say you should enjoy life first and work for your goals second. I also say that if your goal doesn't make you happy, then maybe it's the wrong goal."

"Well, you wouldn't know, would you, because you don't have any real goals," Caroline said icily.

Alex got to his feet and looked Caroline in the eye. "How would you know, Caroline?" he asked quietly. "One hundred percent of your time is wrapped up in you. I was willing to take second place to you because I could see you needed all the support you could get, but I'm not willing to wait around forever, just remember that. I'm a person, too, Caroline. I have feelings of my own." He turned, walked to the front door, and shut it quietly behind him.

Caroline stood staring down the empty hallway as if she were made of stone. She found that she was shivering, even though the apartment was warm. In the several wonderful months they had been dating, she and Alex had never had a real fight. Sure, they'd disagreed a few times, and even had a major misunderstanding, but never this—a real attempt to hurt each other with words. Somehow it was even more terrible that Alex had not lost his cool. He hadn't raised his voice once, and hadn't stormed out. She was the one who'd blown up, and the worst thing of all was that Alex had been totally right. She had never thought of his feelings. He was always Alex, who would be there to give her support when she needed it most. She didn't know what his dreams were. She didn't even go to cheer at his soccer games.

I deserve to lose him, she thought, feeling the great weight of despair settling on her. *I've been so wrapped up in my own problems that I haven't had time to think of anyone else. Surely Alex understands that. I must talk to him in the morning and make him understand that I really do love him and that I'll make time for him . . . if I can just get through this horrible contest first. . . .*

As she undressed, Caroline remembered her math homework, which she hadn't even started. *Oh well,* she thought, *I suppose I'll have to get up extra early tomorrow.* Just the thought made her more tired and depressed. She climbed into bed, curling into a tight little ball and pulling her comforter over her head, to shut out the world. Alex's words continued to nag her. What did she really want? Did she really want to win the contest and be a professional ballerina? Did ballet make her happy?

I wish I knew, she murmured over and over. *I wish I knew what I really wanted.*

One thing was certain, though: She definitely wanted Alex. *Why did I say such terrible things to him?* she asked herself. *I really hurt his feelings badly, and I didn't mean to. If only I can make it all right again tomorrow. . . .*

"Oh, Alex," she whispered into her pillow. "What would I do without you?" Before she could stop them, tears started to well up in her eyes. The exhaustion and the tension and the horrible empty fear of losing Alex all came flooding out in a torrent of sobs. She was glad for once that Chrissy was out at Tracy's house, because these were tears she knew she couldn't stifle. She cried and cried until she fell into an uneasy sleep.

Caroline hurried to school the next morning, determined to catch Alex before he went to his first class. When she saw him walking down the hall toward her, his hands in his pockets, his dark hair falling forward the way it always did, a lump came to her throat and she had the horrible feeling she might cry again at any moment. As he drew level with her, he gave her an almost shy little smile.

"Hi, Cara," he said, and started to walk on.

Caroline quickly stepped in front of him. "Alex," she pleaded. "Can you talk for a minute? I just wanted to say about last night—"

"It's okay," Alex said hastily. Caroline thought he must be embarrassed to talk about their personal relationship in the middle of a crowded hallway, the way his eyes kept darting from the floor to the ceiling. "I understand what you're going through, Cara. You're under a lot of stress. I know that."

"But I want to tell you how sorry I am," Caroline insisted. "I said some very mean things to you. I didn't mean them, Alex."

"It's okay," Alex said again. "I guess I pushed you too far."

"You're very important to me, Alex. I want

everything to be all right between us. Just give me some time. I'll sort things out," she begged.

Alex managed a smile and put his hand gently on her arm. "Don't worry about it, okay?" He looked up uneasily. "Look, I have to go. I have a test in physics and I didn't study enough last night. I'll see you, Cara."

And he was gone. Caroline walked over to her locker and began stuffing things mechanically into her book bag. Alex had seemed as sweet and gentle as always. He'd been understanding about last night, but Caroline sensed that something was wrong. Maybe it was the way he had avoided looking at her, or the way he had put his hand on her arm, but Caroline definitely sensed a distance that had not been there before, as if she'd crossed a bridge during the night and was now talking to him from the other side of a ravine.

As the day of the Halloween party neared, Caroline made a huge effort to show more enthusiasm. She wanted Alex to see that she could still have fun, and hoped the party would give them a chance to go back to the way they used to be—when they'd had time to laugh and talk together. They would dance to the soft music, Alex would hold her tightly in his arms, and they would remember just how much they meant to each other. . . .

On Halloween night Caroline had rehearsal, as usual. The dancers made jokes to each other that

Madame would call rehearsals on Christmas Day and Fourth of July without batting an eyelash. Caroline felt guilty that by the time she came home, the whole apartment was already decorated and the food all prepared. Chrissy and Tracy had done wonders with the apartment. Huge black cobwebs drifted across the front hall, making all the guests scream as they entered. Helium balloons draped in sheets rose to the ceiling and wafted around, looking like very realistic ghosts. Bowls of dry ice in the corners sent a low, swirling mist across the room and jack-o'-lanterns grinned with twisted, tormented candlelit faces.

Pretty soon the apartment was crammed full of monsters, witches, and every other sort of creature—mostly kids from the play, and some guys from the football team who never missed a party. The kids from the play were all loud and lively under normal circumstances, but when the football players—disguised as creepy monsters—began running around with cardboard axes and slurping cold spaghetti guts, everyone giggled hysterically.

Only Caroline sat in the middle of the chaos, feeling that she had just landed from Mars. She smiled politely when people smiled at her, and spoke when they spoke to her, but she couldn't get into their spirit of crazy, uninhibited fun.

Maybe it's a good thing I left the play when I did, she kept telling herself, *because I'm not like these people. They would have thought I was boring and stuffy. Perhaps I am.*

"Ah, Caroline, my beautiful—would you care for a sip of my blood? It's a very good vintage," Alex said, swirling his Dracula cape around her and handing her a glass of red liquid.

"Yuk! Alex, that's disgusting," Caroline said, pushing the glass away from her face.

"Hey, come on, get into the spirit of things," Alex said, pulling on her arm. "Come through the haunted room and feel the lovely guts and eyeballs."

"Thanks, but I'll play it safe and stay right here," Caroline replied, hoping the smile on her witch's face looked real.

But clearly she didn't fool Alex. "You're not having much fun, are you?" he asked.

"I'm trying to get into the spirit, but I can't," she replied. "Something inside me says that I know the guts are only cold spaghetti, so what's the big deal? Do you think I'm the only person who has outgrown Halloween?"

"I think you're the only person who has forgotten what a good time means," Alex said, looking at her with dark, serious eyes.

"Oh, come on, Alex," Caroline said, feeling her cheeks flushing. "You can't tell me that cold spaghetti and cobwebs and eyeballs are your idea of a good time!"

Alex frowned. "Sometimes it's fun to be a kid again," he said. "I'm having a terrific time. It's too bad you're not." Then he turned away with a swish of his cape.

"Alex!" Caroline called after him. "I'll come to the haunted room if that's what you really want." But he didn't turn around. "And I am trying to have fun," she continued in a small voice that got lost in the racket.

The party got even louder and wilder. Nancy Chin, one of the chorus dancers, ran past screaming in a harem costume, followed by one of the huge football linebackers who was attempting to drop one of the "eyeballs" down her back.

It's not that I don't want to join in. I'd like to be laughing and screaming, too, but I just can't, Caroline thought. She caught a glimpse of Alex giving a horrible monster laugh as he pursued Jan with an "eyeball." The pretty redheaded dancer, now dressed as a fortune teller, screamed in delight and ran away just slowly enough so Alex could drop the grape down her back.

Caroline walked over to the punchbowl and helped herself to another glass. *I'll be overdosing on ginger ale soon,* she thought grimly. Jan and Nancy came up to join her, both breathing heavily.

"I still have that grape down my back," Nancy was saying. "I've got to get into the bathroom and find it. It feels horrible!" But she was laughing as she said it.

"I'll come with you," Jan agreed, "and you can help find mine. I'd hate to sit on it!" They both exploded into peels of laughter.

"How come you've managed to escape so far?" Nancy asked, noticing Caroline for the first time.

"She's smart," Jan said, smiling at Caroline. "Real ballet dancers like her can just escape with one giant leap!"

"I hear you had to quit the musical to enter a national contest or something?" Nancy asked, pouring herself a glass of punch.

Caroline nodded.

"You must be very good," Nancy went on.

"Of course she's very good," Jan answered for her. "You could see the way she danced with us. We only had real easy steps to do, but she showed all of us up doing those. She just lifted her leg above her head when we were all groaning at getting it waist high." She turned to Caroline. "I'd better get your autograph right now, before you come back from the competition all famous and don't want to know us anymore."

"Oh, come on, Jan," Caroline squirmed with embarrassment. "I haven't even been chosen officially to represent my school yet, and there will be girls from all over the country competing. I don't have much chance of winning, you know."

"You're too modest," Jan said. "Your cousin Chrissy was telling us that she overheard your parents talking about moving to New York for when you get accepted by the ballet there."

"Wow, New York," Nancy said excitedly. "You lucky thing. I'd love to go there. Will you be finishing up high school here first?"

"The scholarship is just for a summer session," Caroline mumbled. Somehow she was finding it hard to make her tongue obey her. "But they invite the best students to stay on as apprentices."

"Good for you," Nancy said. "I really admire your dedication."

"Me, too," Jan agreed. "I know I could never keep practicing day in and day out, giving up all the fun things in high school. You really deserve all your success, Caroline."

They moved away, leaving Caroline alone with her glass of punch. Her hand around the glass was trembling, and not just with the cold of the liquid. It seemed that everyone else already had her winning the contest and being a famous ballerina. Even her parents were already talking of moving to New York. They all expected her to succeed. How would she face them all if she failed? What if she wasn't even one of the ones chosen from her own school? She felt almost sick with fright. The room was suddenly too warm. Her skin felt clammy and it was hard to breathe. She pushed her way past a group of dancing ghouls, past a witch and a devil in very close consultation, and opened the door onto the little balcony off the kitchen.

As she was about to step out onto the terrace, she noticed that it was already occupied. Caroline could clearly see Dracula and the fortune teller standing very close together in the moonlight. Their breath was rising like steam in the crisp night air. It only took a very brief glance for Caroline to realize that the fortune teller was not telling his fortune.

Chapter 7

"Again! Do it again! Go back and do it again!" Madame's voice bounced off the mirrored walls. After an hour of class she was the only person who showed no sign of failing strength—she was still yelling as loudly as when they had started, and thumping her stick so violently that the floorboards quivered. Caroline could feel sweat trickling down between her shoulder blades and collecting on the waistband of her tights. It was dripping down her face so freely that she had trouble keeping it out of her eyes.

Caroline made herself work as hard as she could, pumping her leg up and down so that every ounce of her energy was put toward dancing. She didn't want any energy left for thought, because if she started thinking, she knew she'd dwell upon the awful fight she'd just had with Chrissy. But even as she tried to concentrate on dancing, Caroline kept replaying the scene in her mind.

Chrissy had come into the room as Caroline was packing her ballet bag. She hadn't said anything right away, which was unusual for Chrissy. Normally she burst in yelling as soon as she opened the front door. Caroline stuffed a clean leotard on top of her shoes and a clean towel on top of the leotard.

"Caroline," Chrissy said at last, "do you have a minute? I'd like to talk to you."

Caroline looked up. "What is it?" she asked. The words had come out harshly although she hadn't intended them to.

Chrissy's face flushed under Caroline's sharp stare. "I just wondered if . . . I mean if you knew about—Caroline, Alex came to our rehearsal today."

Caroline's heart skipped a beat at the mention of his name. She could feel her nails digging into her clenched palms, willing Chrissy to say what she wanted to hear. She fought to keep her face calm.

"So?" she asked.

"So I thought he might have forgotten that you had quit. I asked him if he'd come to pick you up, but he blushed bright red and mumbled something and walked out again. A couple of minutes later Jan came running up and looked around as if she expected somebody to be there." There was a pause. Caroline could feel the blood thudding in her temples. She knew Chrissy was expecting her to say something, but she couldn't make any words come out.

"I couldn't help wondering, Cara," Chrissy said gently, "if Alex came to pick up Jan."

"So?" Caroline asked again, feeling her head dangerously near to exploding.

"Do you have to keep saying that?" Chrissy asked. "So maybe I'm jumping to conclusions, but I thought that you should know about it."

"What for?" Caroline asked bluntly.

"So that you can do something, Cara, before it's too late. You love Alex, don't you? Well, I've seen him around school talking to Jan. I've seen the way she looks at him. You've got to do something, Cara."

"Like what?" Caroline snapped. "Kill Jan? Kill Alex? Kill myself?"

"Just go talk to him," Chrissy pleaded. "Tell him you'll make more time for him—tell him you want him back."

"Oh, sure," Caroline said bitterly. "That's bound to do it. I don't see how I can compete with a bouncy little cheerleader who has all the time in the world, and what's more, is chasing very hard. I don't have much experience of these things you know. I don't know how to chase a boy."

"Then you'd better learn pretty quick if you want to hang on to this one," Chrissy said. "If I were you, I'd even skip a few dance classes to make time for Alex. He's worth fighting for, Cara."

"What are you talking about?" Caroline demanded, her voice rising dangerously. "I mean, mon Dieu, you haven't the slightest idea, do you? Skip a few dance classes and have everyone yelling at me nonstop—oh, that's great."

"It depends how much your boyfriend means to you," Chrissy said uneasily. "I know I'd do anything to fight for Ben."

Caroline's eyes narrowed. "Yes, well, you don't have much else in life besides a boyfriend, do you? You don't have any special talent—"

"I got the solo in the musical," Chrissy retorted, "so I can't be too bad, can I?"

"Just get out!" Caroline shouted. "I have to share my room with you—I have to share my life with you—but I don't have to put up with you giving me your wonderful advice on how to keep my boyfriend. Just get this clear—I don't want your advice. Let me live my own life and make my own mistakes. Just butt out, Chrissy."

"I only wanted to help," Chrissy said, following Caroline around the room as she shut her closet and pulled on her jacket. "I just wanted to help you get Alex back."

"I bet you did," Caroline said icily. "I have to go. I'll be late for my ballet school. I have the small matter of a national competition to think about!"

As she played that scene through again, word for word in her head, she felt hot all over with embarrassment. How could she have said such mean things to Chrissy? She knew that Chrissy would not tell her something just to hurt her. She really did want to help get Alex and Caroline back together again.

But the trouble is, Caroline thought as she turned to repeat the exercise, *that nobody can help me. I've got to get Alex back on my own.*

"What do you wait for?" Madame's voice cut through her thoughts and brought her back to the reality of the ballet lesson. "No sleeping allowed in my class. Begin again. *And* one, *and* two . . ." The music began again, and eight left legs rose and fell. Caroline took a quick glance at the other students. Were they all as tired as she was? Were their legs still lifting effortlessly when she felt that she needed a crane to get hers to hip height?

Beside her she could see Tais, looking petite and frail as she stared straight ahead and bit her lip in concentration. Caroline turned her head a little to look harder at Tais, and noticed a bead of sweat on her friend's bottom lip. Tais's face was normally the color of a porcelain doll, but today it was flushed, almost matching the bright pink of her leotard. Caroline faced front again, comforted that even Tais was finding these workouts strenuous. Usually Tais floated across the floor as if gravity had no meaning for her.

"Once more, other leg," Madame commanded. Caroline forced the other leg to obey her, counting hopefully: *Only ten more to go, only nine more to go, only eight . . .*

"And relax," Madame commanded. "Five minutes, zen we begin our serious work."

Some girls just slumped to the floor where they were, and one or two made for the water fountain in the hall. Caroline stumbled over to her towel and attempted to mop off her face. Tais came up beside her and began drying her face silently.

"Isn't this fun?" Caroline whispered sarcastically. "Do you sometimes wonder if she was a guard in a prison camp before she became a ballet teacher."

"She has to get us in shape if we want to represent her in the contest," Tais said, panting as she spoke.

Again Caroline looked at her. "Are you okay?" she asked. "You don't look too good."

"Neither do you, with your hair plastered down with sweat," Tais said, attempting to joke.

"You know what I mean, Tais," Caroline said. "I mean you don't look well. Your face is really red."

"Actually I don't feel too good," Tais admitted. "I'm fighting off this flu."

"It doesn't look to me as if you're fighting it off too well," Caroline said. She reached over and put her hand on her friend's forehead. "You're burning up," she said.

"I'm okay. It's a hard practice," Tais mumbled.

"I think you should go home and rest up," Caroline said with concern. "You shouldn't be exhausting yourself like this when you're running a fever."

"How can I afford to miss a practice right now?" Tais snapped. She got to her feet and began to do stretches, bringing her face down toward her knee. "We only have three weeks before the competition, you know. I just can't afford to be sick."

She walked away from Caroline, back to the center of the floor, and stood in fifth position, ready to dance again.

"To your places," Madame commanded, clapping her hands. "We will run through zee second section of zee routine. Begin with zee grand jetés en tournant."

She would have to pick the second section, Caroline thought, walking to take her place at the back of the room. *That's the hardest part of the whole routine.*

Loud, lively music from a Beethoven sonata filled the room. "Keep zee tempo up, and begin," Madame commanded, cueing them in. The dancers leaped across the floor.

"No! *No! No!*" Madame yelled. The pianist broke off, looking up timidly.

"Again! Do it again!" Madame thumped the floor with her stick. "And zis time put your soul into it. I do not wish to see sacks of potatoes turning. I wish to see ballet dancers. Begin!"

Again they leaped across the floor. Again Madame sent them back. The room was beginning to spin around for Caroline, and she heard a faint singing in the back of her head. She didn't dare ask to rest because she knew what Madame would say. Madame had already said it to one student: "If you feel you are not ready to prepare for zis competition, zen kindly leave zee class and go back to your regular lesson." Caroline gulped in air and forced her legs across the room yet again. She snatched another quick look at Tais as she turned. Tais was still staring straight ahead of her, dancing like a robot.

How can she dance when she's sick? Caroline wondered. *It's as if she's made of steel.*

"Now we go on with zee entrechats," Madame commanded. *More leaps, more runs, more turns—only half an hour to go,* Caroline thought as she watched Tais begin a leap in front of her. Then, without warning, Tais crumpled like a falling leaf to the floor. She lay in a little pink heap, graceful even when unconscious. The girls started to run toward her, but Madame banged her stick.

"She is not zee first person who has fainted during practice. I myself often used to faint when I practiced at six in zee morning with no breakfast first. Caroline, help her to zee side of zee room. Zee rest of you, continue."

The stick thumped. The music began again. Caroline put her arms around Tais and dragged her to the side of the room. She was surprisingly light to move. As Caroline leaned her against the cool wall, Tais opened her eyes and looked around like a startled fawn.

"What happened?"

"You fainted," Caroline said. "I kept telling you that you were sick. Now will you go home?"

"I guess," Tais said. "I feel all shivery."

"Here." Caroline pulled her own sweater from the bench and put it around Tais. "How do you get home? Does someone pick you up?"

"On the streetcar," Tais said. "I'll be okay."

"Can you phone your folks to come get you?" Caroline asked.

"There's nobody home. I live with my dad, and he's not there."

Caroline thought how fragile Tais looked, and knew she couldn't leave her on her own. "Look, Tais, I don't think you should go home alone. What if you passed out on the street? I'll come with you."

"You don't have to do that," Tais said. "You shouldn't miss practice because of me."

"I'm prepared to make that sacrifice," Caroline said with a grin. "Two more minutes and I would have joined you in a crumpled heap. Do you feel strong enough to stand yet?"

"I think so," Tais said, and got slowly to her feet.

"Good. You are recovered. Back to your place," Madame commanded, as if nothing unusual had happened.

Caroline looked at Madame in amazement. "Tais is very sick, Madame," she said firmly. "She's burning up with fever, so I'm going to take her home."

She didn't wait for Madame's reply. Instead she

put her arm around Tais's tiny waist and helped her from the room.

Tais seemed to be a little stronger in the cold night air, but on the streetcar, packed in like sardines, she slumped against Caroline's shoulder. Caroline could hear her breathing even above the noise of the crowded car. And when the girls reached Tais's house, her fingers shook as she tried to fit the key into the lock. Caroline took it from her and opened the door.

"What time will your dad be back?" she asked, helping Tais inside.

"He won't," Tais said, neatly hanging her coat in the hall closet. "He's a pilot. I think he's on the Australia run this week."

Caroline looked around the hallway, taking in the cold marble floor, the elegant Chinese chest, and Oriental rugs scattered here and there. She peered through an open door into the immaculate living room with a brilliant white carpet, a white leather sofa, and a bookcase filled with books which looked as if they were only there for decoration. It was more like an expensive furniture showroom than a home, Caroline thought.

Tais finished hanging up her coat. "Well, thanks for bringing me home," she said shyly. "I don't know if I would have made it without you. I'd probably have fallen asleep on the streetcar and be out at the ocean by now."

"Will you be okay?" Caroline asked with concern.

"Oh, sure. I'll get myself something to eat and go to bed," Tais said. "Don't worry, I'll be fine."

"But when does your father get home? Don't you have any other relatives around you could call?"

Tais shrugged her shoulders indifferently. "I think he's due back on Friday," she said, "and the rest of my family live in Nevada."

Caroline thought briefly of the chemistry assignment and the history test scheduled for the next morning, but decided Tais was more important. "You go straight to bed," she ordered her friend. "I'll fix you something hot to eat, then you can sleep."

"You don't have to do that—" Tais began.

But Caroline cut her short. "I'm going to," she said. "Now show me where the kitchen is, then go get into bed."

Tais gave her a grateful smile. "Boy, I didn't know you could be so bossy," she said. "You always seem so nice and sweet in ballet class. You never talk back when Madame yells at you. . . ." She began to walk wearily down the hall. "The kitchen's through here," she said, pointing to a closed white door, "and my bedroom's up these stairs."

Caroline let herself into the kitchen. It looked as though it had never been used. Did Tais really live here? she wondered. She couldn't help thinking of her own apartment. Her father always scattered his newspapers across the living room, and her mother usually kept a variety of paintings and sculptures around the apartment from the art gallery where she worked. The Kirbys' apartment also contained lots of well-worn books and sentimental knickknacks that made it special. *Poor Tais,* Caroline thought. *She doesn't even have a home.*

Rummaging through the fridge and the cupboards, she found an assortment of useless things like cans of paté and a bottle of Worcestershire sauce, but nothing she could give to Tais. The freezer was stuffed with diet frozen dinners which Caroline knew didn't taste as good as they looked on the boxes. Finally she found a can of chicken noodle soup and heated that up, then made a pitcher of frozen lemonade in case Tais's throat was bothering her the way Caroline's always did when she had a cold.

She carried the tray up the white-carpeted stairs and tiptoed into Tais's room, where she stopped in the doorway, staring with amazement. Against one wall there was a single bed and a desk, but no other furniture in the room, and no carpet. The opposite wall was mirrored with a barre running the full length of it. Tais's bed looked as though it had been placed in a dance studio by mistake.

"Wow," Caroline said. "You told me you had a practice room at home, but I had no idea—"

"I do an hour every morning before school," Tais said, wriggling to sit up in bed. "Sometimes I try to squeeze in an hour before I go to sleep, too."

Caroline said nothing, but put the tray in front of Tais.

"Gee, thanks, this looks wonderful," Tais said, beaming at Caroline as if it were a feast.

"I'm sorry, but the chicken soup was the only thing in the kitchen that I thought you might feel like eating," Caroline said, sitting down on the end of the bed. "I would have boiled you an egg as well. . . ."

Tais gave a short laugh. "We don't go in for food too much," she said. "My father usually eats out, and I stick to stuff like yogurt. I'm always watching my weight. You know how it is."

"I'm sure you don't need to watch your weight," Caroline said firmly. "You are about the skinniest person I know."

"Only because I diet all the time," she said. "Hey, this tastes delicious."

"But I don't think you should diet too much," Caroline said cautiously. "I tried that for a while and I almost got sick. You can't fight off germs if you have no food to give you energy."

"It's not lack of food," Tais said. "I guess I've been doing too much with this scholarship contest, you know. I've been putting in a lot of extra practice. . . ."

Caroline looked hard at her. "You really want this badly, don't you?" she asked.

Tais's face lit up. Her cheeks had been flushed and her eyes fever-bright before, but now she positively glowed. "I want it more than anything in the world," she said. "I've been aiming to dance in New York all my life, and now I'm almost there. My father has even promised to get me an apartment there if I'm accepted—"

"Won't you mind being away from home?" Caroline blurted out, then realized what a dumb thing she had said.

Tais looked at her steadily. "What home?" she asked. "I'm here alone most of the time anyway. If I wanted home, I could have stayed with my mother."

"In Nevada?" Caroline asked.

Tais nodded. "She went back to her folks after the divorce. They have a big ranch there. She took my little brother with her. . . ." Caroline noticed the wistful tone in her voice.

"And your father got custody of you?" she asked.

Tais shook her head. "I chose to be with him," she said. "I had to stay in San Francisco for my training. I couldn't leave Madame, could I?"

Caroline thought privately that if she had to choose between her family and Madame, Madame would come in a poor second.

Tais gave a little sigh. "It's not easy to be us, is it?" she asked. "Other people don't understand that we have to give up everything to be professional ballerinas."

Caroline looked across the bare room. She could see her own face staring back at her from the mirrored wall. *But I'm not prepared to give up everything,* she realized.

Tais finished the soup and put down her spoon. "That was really great, Caroline," she said. "I feel much better now. You don't have to hang around any longer. I think I'll be able to sleep this off by morning."

"Look, you stay in bed tomorrow," Caroline ordered. "You are not going to be well enough to come to ballet class. I'll try to drop by after school, and you've got my phone number if you need me."

"Thanks a million, but I'll be fine," Tais said. "All I need is sleep."

She snuggled down under her white comforter, looking more like a china doll than ever. Caroline took the tray, left the pitcher of lemonade, and crept from the room.

An icy wind swept down the avenue as she walked toward the streetcar stop. The bare branches of the mulberry trees creaked as they swayed above her head, reminding Caroline of the skeleton she had seen dancing at the Halloween party on Friday. The thought of the party made Caroline think of Alex, and she felt a sharp sense of foreboding. Just then, the wind hit Caroline full in the face, like a slap. But she didn't mind. She'd finally figured out what Alex had known all the time—that she, Caroline Kirby, did not want to be a famous ballerina.

I'm not like Tais, she thought. *She's a real ballerina. She wants to be a dancer more than anything. I wouldn't mind if Madame phoned tomorrow and said there were no more classes—* She broke off, horrified at what had just passed through her mind. Was that true, she wondered? Would she really not care if there were no more dance classes in her life—ever? Would she really not care if she didn't become a ballerina? She thought of the competition. How would she feel if she didn't win one of the scholarships? She would feel bad about letting other people down, of course, but for herself?

I don't want to go to New York next summer, she thought. *I'm not ready to move away from home the way Tais is. . . . I'm not even sure that I want to join a ballet company at all.* In her mind, Caroline weighed the advantages of a career in ballet against the disadvantages, and decided that she had been right a moment ago—she no longer wanted to be a ballerina.

Now that she had admitted this to herself, she felt strangely calm and comforted, as if she'd been making a great effort to stop the thought from forming earlier. *I don't have to be a dancer,* she told herself. *Alex was right. I don't have to do anything I don't want to.*

Caroline reached the streetcar stop and stepped back into a doorway to escape the full force of the wind. *The big problem,* she told herself, *is convincing everybody else that I don't have to be a dancer if I don't want to. . . .*

Chapter 8

The next day Caroline stood beside her locker, debating whether she had time during the lunch period to rush over to see Tais again. She had gone before school that morning, and Tais had still been far from well, and very weak. Caroline had left her with hot tea and toast, but had worried about her all morning. She thought of herself when she was sick, and how horrible it would be to have no one to look after her. Caroline's mother always knew what foods to tempt her with and brought cool towels for her face. What would she do without her?

Thinking about Tais, who had no family to care for her, had definitely decided Caroline against going to New York. As Caroline put away her books and took out her lunch bag, she thought,

I'm not ready to leave the nest yet!

She decided with regret that she'd never make it to Tais's house and back in forty-five minutes, then turned from her locker to see Alex standing beside her. "Oh, hi," she stammered, feeling herself blushing as she glanced up at him uneasily.

Since that night at the party, Caroline hadn't had a chance to talk to him. She was pretty sure he'd left with Jan that night, and she'd seen him talking to Jan a couple of times around school, but hadn't dared to confront him about it. She could keep hoping, as long as she didn't know for sure.

"Hi, Cara," Alex greeted her with a smile. "Rushing off for a rehearsal or something?"

"Just going to eat my lunch," she answered cautiously.

"Mind if I join you?" he asked.

"Sure, why not?"

"How about we walk up to the park—I'd like to talk," Alex said.

"Fine with me," Caroline replied, trying to keep her voice calm and even.

As they walked down the front steps side by side, Caroline wrestled with the fear that was tying her stomach into a tight knot. She forced herself not to look at Alex. *What does he want to talk about?* she asked herself. *Dumb question—obviously about us!*

She dared to sneak a quick glance at him. He was walking along easily enough, with his usual big, relaxed strides. *Maybe I'm panicking for nothing,* she thought. *Maybe everything will be just fine.* After all, Alex had smiled at her when he saw her. He had sounded like his old self—warm and easygoing. Caroline didn't know what to think. *Maybe he wants to tell me he's sorry for going off with Jan like that,* she thought hopefully.

They turned the corner and began to climb the steep hill to the park. As they climbed higher, they met the full force of the wind.

"Are you sure you want to eat lunch up here? We'll be blown away," Caroline said, gasping as the wind snatched her breath away.

"I want to be alone with you," he said. "There never seems to be a chance."

He wants to be alone with me, she thought happily, repeating the words in her head.

"I've been really busy," she said.

"I've noticed. I tried to call your house about three times, but you were never there."

"We've had extra dance practices for this competition."

"That's what Chrissy told me."

They climbed higher in silence. On this windswept, gray fall day the little park was deserted. Even the walls lining two sides of the park and the big magnolia trees clustered on the green were poor shelter against the wind from the ocean. The smaller trees groaned and creeked in protest, and dried leaves scurried down sandy paths. Alex sat on a bench next to the high brick wall and Caroline sat beside him, still nervous. They both opened their lunch bags.

"Tuna!" Alex exclaimed. "I hate tuna."

Caroline was tempted to offer him her roast beef sandwich, but she sensed that he had only said that to ease the uncomfortable silence. *We can't talk to each other anymore,* she thought, the scared feeling creeping through her again. *We don't know how to begin. . . .*

They unwrapped their sandwiches and started to eat, while holding down their brown lunch bags against the unrelenting wind.

"Kind of breezy, huh?" Alex said with an attempt at a laugh.

At last Caroline could stand the tension no longer. *If he's not going to say something, I will,* she decided. *I have to find out where we stand.* She took a deep breath, "Look, Alex, about that night—" she began.

At the same time, Alex was saying, "Look, Cara, I wanted to tell you—"

They both broke off, looked at each other and laughed nervously.

"What were you going to say?" Alex asked.

"No, you first," Caroline said.

Alex shifted awkwardly in his seat. "I've been putting this off," he said, "because I wanted to be really sure before I told you. I wanted to find out how I felt about you, and about us. . . ."

There was a long pause. Caroline felt she should say something, but she didn't know what.

"You probably noticed at the Halloween party

. . . " Alex went on, tearing at the edge of his lunch bag and not looking at her.

"I did notice. You went home with Jan."

"Yes, you see I—"

"You don't have to apologize, Alex. You're not married to me or anything," Caroline said. "If you want to talk to other girls, or drive them home, I understand."

Alex coughed uneasily. "I don't think you do understand, Cara," he said. "Jan and I—we've been seeing a lot of each other and . . . well, I felt it was only fair to tell you, and to break up with you officially."

"Oh," was all Caroline managed to say.

Alex coughed again. "I really tried hard, Cara," he said. "I tried to understand what you were going through, but I guess I'm not prepared to play second fiddle to your dancing any longer. I don't want to waste my entire high school years sitting home, hoping my girlfriend will be able to spare me five minutes every now and then. I want a girlfriend who can come cheer at my soccer games sometimes, someone who can sit and talk to me in the evenings and even do homework with me. I really like you a lot, Cara, but you never had time for me. You never will have time for me."

Caroline got to her feet. "I'd better be getting back to school," she said. "I don't want to be late for chemistry."

"You haven't finished your lunch."

"I guess I'm not hungry today," Caroline replied, wondering when she would wake up from this nightmare.

She walked along the narrow sandy path without looking back. It had begun to rain—a fine misty drizzle off the Pacific. She didn't try to wipe the rain out of her face or even zip up her jacket. The rain seemed right for this moment—it matched her mood.

Alex ran after her and grabbed her arm. "Look, Cara, I'm sorry," he said. "I really am sorry, but I hung around for months, hoping that you could juggle your schedule so that you'd have time for me. But you made your decision, and your ballet comes first. Well, I'd like to come first in someone's life. Jan seems to know how to really enjoy herself. She makes me laugh, and I need that right now."

"It's okay, Alex," Caroline said in a clenched voice. "You don't have to go on talking about it. It was nice of you to tell me to my face. I appreciate that."

Alex put a slight pressure on her arm and turned her toward him. "You're a great girl, Caroline," he said. "I wish you luck. You're going to be a terrific ballerina."

Then he released her and ran down the hill ahead of her, back to school. Caroline followed him slowly, letting the wind push her back down the hill.

"Hey, Cara, what were you doing out in that rain?" Tracy asked, hurrying past with an armful of books as Caroline came dripping through the door of the school. "Have you finally flipped? It's cold out there, and you're soaked to the skin."

Maybe I have finally flipped, Caroline thought as she peeled off her wet jacket at her locker. *I've messed up just about everything that matters to me—I hardly ever spend time with my friends anymore, I had a horrible fight with Chrissy, I quit the musical, and now I've lost Alex—and all for something I don't even care about. Maybe I am crazy!*

She walked right past several people without acknowledging their greetings and sat down at her desk in a daze. She could hear the chemistry teacher droning on, but the words meant nothing. All Caroline could think of was Alex. She punished herself by going through all the happy scenes in her mind: the first time he'd asked her out last spring, when they had joined in protesting the destruction of some old houses; the first time he kissed her out on his parents deck, as the fog came in to swallow up the city and wrap them in a private cocoon. She saw Alex trying to cram ten sweaters into his backpack as he left on his hiking trip, and standing shyly by the stage door with an armful of roses after her dance performance.

He was warm and funny and wonderful, and I let him go, she thought over and over again. *How can I have been so dumb? He gave me enough warning. He kept trying to tell me that he wouldn't wait forever. I suppose I thought that two people who cared about each other would never break up. . . .*

She willed herself not to cry. The last three periods seemed to drag on forever. She packed up her math books, sure the teacher had assigned some homework, but she hadn't been listening and didn't care enough to ask. *What does it matter anymore?* she thought, dragging her steps down the hall toward the exit. *I've spent my life working hard for good grades and good ballet dancing, and look where it's gotten me.*

"She makes me laugh," Alex's voice echoed mockingly through her head. How much better to be a cheerleader whose biggest contribution to the world was to leap up and down screaming on the sideline. At least she made people laugh.

Caroline turned her feet toward California Street and her ballet school. Two hours of Madame's yelling and thumping were more than she could bear right now. *I'll just skip today and tell Madame I didn't feel well,* she thought suddenly. *You'll be cut from the tryouts if you do that,* her conscience reminded her. *Look at Tais—she was scared to miss even one day, when she was really sick.*

I'll pretend to be sick and let them cut me, then I won't have to go through with this. Then another, more shocking thought came into her mind. *Why should I pretend? I'll just tell them I want to quit. They can't make me dance. Nobody can force me to dance except me!*

That seemed like a pretty good idea until her conscience took over again, reminding her how disappointed her parents would be.

It's no use, she told herself hopelessly, *I'm trapped. I'm going to have keep on dancing because I'd feel too guilty if I quit. All I can do is pray that I don't do well in the contest. Then my Mom might realize that I'm not going to be a top ballerina after all. . . .*

Caroline reached the ballet school all too quickly and threw down her bag on the changing-room bench.

"Hey, watch where you're throwing things," came a weak voice from the corner. Caroline jumped as somebody moved. Then she noticed Tais sitting huddled among the coats, and frowned in disbelief.

"What on earth are you doing here?" she demanded. "You're far to sick to dance. You were running a fever of one hundred and two this morning!"

"I'll be fine. I can't afford to miss a class. I don't want her to cut me!" Tais said. "Besides, my fever has gone down. I've been sponging myself with ice water all day."

Caroline took a critical look at Tais. Her face was no longer bright pink, it was true. She looked more like a china doll than ever, her face like a Japanese mask with pure white skin and extra bright eyes.

"I really don't think you should be here just because your fever is down," Caroline said, sitting beside Tais on the bench. "Would you like me to tell Madame that you're really sick? I can testify that I took your temperature. Even she must have the remains of a heart buried somewhere."

Tais attempted to smile. "It's okay. I want to dance," she insisted. "I don't want to miss a day. My legs will stiffen up if I lie around in bed."

"Have you been practicing at home today?" Caroline demanded.

Tais looked down at her hands. "Just a little—some stretching. I didn't feel up to much more, but I did sleep this afternoon, so I should be much stronger now."

"I think you're crazy," Caroline said. "I don't think ballet is ever important enough to risk your health for."

"I do," Tais said. She got up and began peeling off her sweatshirt, revealing her black leotard underneath. "Come on, we don't want to be late for class,"

Caroline watched her friend walk ahead. *Look at us*, she thought. *We are both risking everything for this stupid ballet. It can't be worth that much.*

She hurried after Tais. Madame was standing at the front of the room, an imposing figure in black, her small beady eyes missing nothing as students filed in to take their places at the barre.

"Ah, Tais," was all she said as they came in.

She didn't even ask how Tais was feeling or if she should be dancing again so soon, Caroline thought in wonder. *What kind of person is she if she doesn't care about her students?*

Caroline did not greet Madame, and purposely turned her back on her to do her barre stretches.

The class began smoothly enough. They got through the routine barre exercises with no more than the usual amount of criticism. But when they came to the center work, Madame started to pick on Tais.

"Are you falling asleep on your feet? Faster, faster!" she shouted, clapping her hands to increase the tempo. "You, Tais—are you dreaming? Move, move!"

"Sorry, Madame," Tais muttered.

After the second time Caroline intervened. "She's not well, Madame," she said frostily. "She shouldn't have come to class today."

"Nonsense," Madame said. "When I was training in Paris we were never allowed to be sick. One girl danced with pneumonia. We thought nothing strange about zat—it was required. Tais knows zat a ballerina must make herself hard as steel."

"Why don't you go home and rest, Tais?" Caroline asked, touching her friend's arm.

Tais shrugged her off. "I'll be okay," she said. "I have to stay."

"You don't have to stay," Caroline said. "You're not her slave—you're paying her to teach you."

She was amazed at her own words as she said them, but a moment later she wished she'd spoken more softly.

"You have energy to whisper, Caroline," Madame said coldly, "but apparently not energy to do fouettes on time. Go through zem once more. All of you, and zis time I want to zee heads whipping, whipping!"

They began the grueling spins once more. Caroline could feel the blood singing in her head as she flipped round and round. She imagined how awful it must be for Tais to do the exercise with a fever.

"Why are you stopping, Tais?" Madame roared. "Dance, dance!"

Tais began again, but much slower this time. Caroline glanced at her with concern each time she spun around. At last the set finished.

"Terrible, terrible," Madame shouted. "You call yourself a dancer, Tais? You think you are ready for a real ballet? Go back and do it again!"

With that she gave Tais a push. Even knowing Madame's ferocious temper, Caroline couldn't believe she had meant to push so hard. She had caught Tais off balance, and Tais fell over like a young tree and crashed to the ground. There was a horrified silence, then Tais burst into tears.

Caroline dropped to her side. "Are you hurt?" she asked. "Did she hurt you?"

"My ankle," Tais sobbed. "I twisted my ankle."

The other girls looked at each other in shock. Nobody ever cried in ballet school, no matter how mean Madame was. It was a point of honor among the students. And Tais had always seemed to be the bravest of them all.

"Back to work, all of you!" Madame shouted, banging her stick.

Caroline could feel the fury building up inside her and completely overpowering her fear.

"You don't care about us at all, do you?" she said, turning to Madame. "We're not people at all to you. All you want to do is turn us into a bunch of robots like yourself."

"That is enough, Caroline," Madame said, glaring at her. "And Tais, stop that stupid crying. You are not hurt. Move to the side so we can begin again."

"Of course she's hurt," Caroline said, her voice rising dangerously. "She was sick to start with, and now you've hurt her ankle. We all saw you push her—I wouldn't be surprised if her father wanted to sue you!"

"Caroline, I will not have such talk!" Madame boomed. "You will speak to me with respect at all times!"

"You don't deserve respect," Caroline said, getting to her feet.

"Leave zis room immediately," Madame screeched. "How dare you!"

"That's right, I do dare, finally," Caroline retorted. "It's time somebody told you that you're not God!" She bent to Tais, who was sobbing quietly on the floor. "Do you feel well enough to stand? How's your ankle?"

"It will be okay. I don't think it's broken or anything," Tais said. Caroline helped her to her feet. Several other girls assisted, giving frightened glances at Madame over their shoulders.

"I'm going to call for a taxi to take Tais home," Caroline told Madame. "She's going to rest up until she's really well."

"She won't make the competition if she rests," Madame said.

Caroline stared at her defiantly. "She's good enough to make the competition without any help from you," she said, "and what's more, I bet she gets into the best New York ballet. Come on, Tais." She put her arm around her friend's waist and helped her out to the changing room. "Sit there and I'll get a taxi," she said. Tais was still sobbing and didn't protest.

As Caroline turned toward the hall phone, she met Madame, coming toward her.

"I wish you to know I am very upset with your behavior," Madame said, towering over Caroline. "I shall contact your parents and seriously consider whether I want you representing my school in zee contest!"

"Don't worry," Caroline said, "because I don't want to represent you or your school. I quit, as of now!"

"Caroline, what are you saying?" Madame asked. "You can't just quit. What about your future?"

Caroline was pleased to detect a note of worry in Madame's voice. She realized then that Madame didn't want to lose her, and it gave her a great sense of satisfaction. "I don't want to be a dancer, and I certainly don't want a monster like you as a teacher!" she said.

"You ungrateful little wretch, after all I've done for you!" Madame snapped.

"All you've done is make me miserable for all

these years," Caroline said. "Now that I think about it, I've hated it the whole time. I don't know why I didn't quit years ago, because if you're an example of a ballerina, then I never want to be one."

"You never would be one like me—never! You're a nothing. You don't have zee talent or zee guts," Madame retorted.

As Caroline stared up at her, she began to understand why Madame had pushed them all so frenziedly to succeed. She suddenly felt very strong and powerful. "I bet you never were a ballerina in Paris," she said calmly. "I bet the only reason you want us to be prima ballerinas is because that's the only way you'll get to be famous . . . because you never were!"

Madame's eyes glinted. "Get out!" she hissed. "Get out and don't come back!"

"Don't worry," Caroline said. "Nothing in the world would make me come back here. I'm free for the first time in my life!"

She turned and ran back to Tais. "Come on, let's get out of here," she said.

Chapter 9

It was after seven when Caroline put on her jacket to go home. Tais was resting comfortably with a plate of scrambled eggs and some ice cream on a tray in front of her, the TV on, and her ankle propped up with pillows. Her ankle hadn't swelled, and Caroline suspected that shock rather than pain had made Tais cry. She hoped Madame had gotten a shock, too. She'd seen that the mention of being sued had scared Madame. In fact everything she said had scared Madame. It was wonderful and terrifying at the same time to realize that she had power over a powerful adult! All the way to Tais's house in the taxi, Caroline had felt strangely excited, as if she had grown into an enlarged version of herself.

"You're sure you'll be all right now?" she asked,

pausing in the doorway.

Tais beamed at her. "I'll be fine. I want to thank you so much, Caroline." Her smile clouded over. "But what about you? What about those things you said to Madame about quitting? Do you think she'll forgive you and let you come back? I'll tell her you were only defending me, if you like."

"You don't have to," Caroline said. "I meant what I said. I'm not going back, Tais. I'm through with ballet—I've had enough."

Tais looked as shocked as if Caroline had said she were through with life. "But Caroline, you were just about to make it. You might have gotten the scholarship."

Caroline shook her head. "Seeing everything you've gone through has finally convinced me of one thing, Tais. I don't want to make it as a dancer."

"You don't like dancing?" Tais asked, her big dark eyes opening even wider.

Caroline smiled. "I guess I like dancing. I like moving around to music, and I like the feel of being part of a ballet. But I don't like it enough to make it my life. I don't want to go through anymore of this yelling and suffering. I want to find out what being a teenager is all about before it's too late."

"But what will your parents say?" Tais asked. This brought Caroline down to earth with a jolt. What *would* her parents say? Surely Madame would have already phoned them with her side of the story.

"I don't know," she said uneasily. "They'll probably be mad. They had dreams of a big future for me. To hear my mother talk, she's dreamed of me becoming a ballerina since my very first lesson. They'll probably try to talk me into going back again."

"But you won't?" Tais asked.

Caroline shook her head. "I think I've wanted to quit for a long time, only I didn't know how to escape before."

Tais looked at her for a long time in silence. Then she said quietly, "I'll miss you, Caroline. We were just getting to be good friends. I've never really had a friend at ballet school before."

"I'll come and see you, don't worry," Caroline said. "I have to make sure you're eating properly, don't I?"

Tais smiled weakly. "I'd like that."

"I'd better get home or my folks will start sending out search parties."

Tais nodded. " 'Bye, Caroline."

Caroline started to go, then looked back. "My good friends call me Cara," she said.

" 'Bye, Cara," came the small voice from the sofa.

Once Caroline was outside in the cool night air, walking in the direction of her own apartment, the warmth and excitement began to leave her. What had Madame told her parents about her behavior? What had her parents said to Madame? Had they apologized on her behalf and begged

Madame to take her back—at least to practice for the competition? What would she do if they tried to force her to go back?

Caroline nervously gulped down the cold air. She'd never actually fought with her parents before. Of course, they had yelled at each other over not putting the lid on the peanut butter jar and forgetting to turn off the TV, but they'd never had any big arguments. She knew that lots of kids at school had fights with their parents over curfews or driving privileges or drinking at parties, but she'd always found her parents' rules very reasonable. They had also been understanding on the rare occasions when she'd come home at quarter after twelve instead of on the stroke of midnight. Surely they would be understanding now, Caroline thought anxiously. They'd want her to be happy, wouldn't they?

Caroline quickened her steps. *Of course they'll understand,* she told herself. *Look at that time when I got arrested for protesting the construction of that parking lot—they made a fuss to begin with, but they listened to my point of view.*

"Hi, honeybun, is that you?" her mother called as soon as she let herself in the front door. Caroline felt the knot in her stomach tighten. She had hoped to be able to sneak down the hall to her room.

"Yes, it's me," Caroline called back.

"You're late. Were you visiting your sick friend again?" There was nothing in her mother's voice to indicate that she was angry. Caroline cautiously pushed open the living room door.

"Hi, Mom . . . hi, Dad," she said, looking from one to the other to see their reaction. "I took Tais home again."

"She went to class tonight?" her mother asked in surprise. "I thought you said she was running a fever?"

"She was. She didn't want to miss a class."

Mrs. Kirby shook her head and smiled at the same time. "You budding ballerinas—I really admire your dedication. I don't know if I was ever that disciplined at your age. Still, it will certainly pay off."

Again Caroline looked from one parent to the next. It seemed that Madame had not phoned them yet. They both sat relaxed in their armchairs, smiling up at her as if nothing were wrong. Surely they couldn't know.

At least I get to tell them first, Caroline thought, feeling relieved.

She took a deep breath. "Look, Mom, about ballet—" she began.

"Oh, that reminds me," her mother interrupted. "Let me tell you what happened today. I was talking about you to my boss. Julie seems very impressed with this competition. She's been following your progress since you were so high, and she's almost as proud of you as I am—"

"Nobody could be as proud as you are, dear," Mr. Kirby interrupted. He turned to Caroline. "It's all I can do to stop your mother putting up billboards all over the city. She's almost at the stage of grabbing strangers in the street and telling them about you!"

Her mother laughed. "You do exaggerate, Richard," she said, "but I can't help feeling excited right now. Everything Caroline's been working for is finally happening! And guess what my boss wants to do?" she continued before Caroline could answer. "She wants to give you a reception before you go off for the contest. She wants you to dance your competition number at the gallery. We'll clear one end of the main exhibition room so you'll have plenty of space to dance, and we'll set up chairs at the other end for all the guests. Isn't that wonderful? I'm so proud, Caroline. I feel almost as if it's happening to me, I'm so excited for you!" She leaped up from her seat. "I bet you're starving after all that hard work. We've eaten, but I'll put yours in the microwave for you."

"I'm not very hungry," Caroline called after her, but her mother didn't seem to hear.

Chapter 10

What am I going to do? Caroline asked herself hopelessly. Her face stared back at her from her bedroom mirror, its forehead creased with worry lines, its eyes frightened.

Almost a whole week had gone by and still her parents didn't know the truth. Caroline knew that Madame had not phoned, because her parents continued to treat her with their normal, relaxed friendliness and asked her every night how her ballet class was going.

Every day she felt worse and worse about lying—like a laboratory mouse trapped in a maze. Whichever direction she chose to run in, she knew there was no way out. Now, even if her parents forgave her for quitting ballet school, Caroline doubted that they would forgive her for deceiving them.

Why couldn't I have told them that first evening? she thought bleakly. *It would have been all over and forgotten by now.*

If only her mother hadn't been so proud and excited. It had seemed really cruel at the time to pop her bubble when she was floating so wonderfully. *I'll wait until tomorrow, when she's gotten over the excitement of this reception,* Caroline had decided that evening. But the next evening her parents went out to a concert, and the evening after that her mother was flourishing a guest list for the reception.

"I'll have to tell them soon," she said to the face in the mirror. "I can't let Mom invite all those people to see me dance." *If only I could find the right moment,* she thought. *If only I had someone to talk to about it. . . .*

But there was nobody. Alex would have been perfect—he would have understood why she didn't come right out with the truth. He probably would have even made her laugh about being so dumb. But Caroline had seen Alex walking around school holding hands with Jan Blackman. Everytime she saw them, she turned the other way.

Tais would have listened quietly, but she just couldn't understand why Caroline wanted to quit ballet.

Caroline thought of Tracy next. They had been friends since grade school, but now it seemed that Tracy was best friends with Chrissy. Caroline only caught glimpses of her as she rushed to play rehearsal or left with Chrissy for the pizza parlor. True, they invited Caroline along whenever they saw her, but Caroline always sensed that they did it out of politeness.

I should be able to talk to Chrissy, she told herself. *After all, Chrissy is like a sister.* The trouble was that she already knew what Chrissy would say, and after their fight last week, Caroline didn't want to push her luck. Chrissy was so straightforward and honest herself that she would think Caroline was terrible for deceiving her parents. *So she wouldn't even be on my side,* Caroline thought sadly. *Right now there's nobody on my side.*

She glanced at the clock. Four-thirty. Chrissy was still at play rehearsal at school. In half an hour Caroline knew she would have to leave the house and stay out of sight for two hours, pretending to be at ballet class. So far she'd managed to carry it off, coming home looking suitably exhausted and answering questions about what Madame had said. In fact deceiving her parents was all too easy. Every night she felt as if she would choke with guilt as her mother greeted her warmly and went to heat up her dinner.

But it was harder to deceive Chrissy. Chrissy always seemed to be around at the wrong moment, and she was the sort of person who came right out and asked questions. Caroline was beginning to get so paranoid about slipping out of the house that Chrissy's normally lively and curious behavior started to bug her. During the past few days she had the feeling that Chrissy was spying on her.

"Are you off to ballet class?" Chrissy had asked the day before, catching Caroline as she crept toward the door.

Caroline had jumped. "You know I'm off to ballet class," she'd snapped. "Where else would I be going?"

Chrissy had laughed. "Hold your horses," she'd said. "Anyone would think you had a guilty secret to hide. Are you sure you're not sneaking off to meet some mysterious boy?"

She was clearly joking, but Caroline realized that Chrissy would soon suspect something if she continued to jump at her questions. She decided to start eating her lunch in a corner where Chrissy wouldn't find her, but the very day she put her plan into practice, she found Chrissy and Tracy waiting beside her locker. All through lunch they asked her questions about ballet and the competition, and she'd wondered whether they were trying to trip her up.

Caroline knew she would give herself away sooner or later. *I can't go on like this much longer,* she thought. *I thought when I quit ballet classes that I'd be free, but I'm more trapped than ever. . . .*

She put away her school things—including the

homework she found so hard to concentrate on—
and got out her ballet bag. Outside the rain
pelted the window with bullet-hard drops—one
of the first storms of winter. Caroline looked up at
the sound of a hard gust of wind. Where could
she go tonight? A few nights ago, she'd walked
along Fisherman's Wharf, feeling secure among
anonymous tourists. On another night she had
browsed in the elegant stores around Union
Square, keeping well clear of the ballet school.
But neither the wharf nor the square were inviting prospects on a night like this.

*If only I didn't have to go out. This is a good
excuse to be brave and tell them the truth!* she
decided as the ring of the telephone interrupted
her thoughts. *Great! That's probably Mom. I can
break it to her on the phone. Much easier than
having to face her. . . .*

"Caroline?" Not her mother's voice.

"Yes?"

"Julie Danford, how are you?"

Her mother's boss. The last person in the world
she wanted to speak to right now. "Fine, thank
you."

"That's great. So how are you these days?
You've been so busy, I haven't seen you in ages."

*Now she's going to want to discuss the recep-
tion she's planning to give me,* Caroline thought
in a panic, *and I'm going to have to lie some
more. . . .* She took a deep breath: "Fine, thank
you," she said again. *I'm beginning to sound like
a parrot,* she thought.

"That's great. Listen, I told your mother I'd phone you because she's still setting up that showing at a client's house and she may be running late. I'm going over to bring her home. Maybe I'll see you later!"

"Sure. Thanks. 'Bye."

"You sound like you're in a hurry as usual. Rushing off somewhere?"

"Right."

There was a slight pause at the other end, as if Julie was going to say something, then thought twice about it. Finally she said, "I'll let you go then, hon. 'Bye," and Caroline heard the line go dead.

Caroline picked up her ballet bag. Now she *had* to go out. She couldn't risk being home if Mom brought Julie Danford up to the apartment. She couldn't explain things in front of Julie. It would make Mom look like a fool.

She pulled on her parka, flung the ballet bag over her shoulder, and went out into the rain. It was quite dark outside, and the rain seemed wetter and colder than any rain she ever remembered. She wandered toward the downtown area, dodging spouts of water which cascaded from gutters and trying to defend herself against the huge gusts of wind that threatened to sweep her into the bay. Within ten minutes she was thoroughly soaked and thoroughly miserable.

I can't do this for two hours, Caroline thought. As she reached Sutter Street she found herself battling the army of commuters charging out of their offices, with heads bent under open umbrellas. After narrowly missing a spike in the eye, she finally took refuge in a little corner coffee bar. She bought a cup of hot chocolate and seated herself on a stool by the steamy window. Gradually the hot liquid began to thaw out her fingers, and the glow spread through her whole body. She wiped a clear area in the window and peeked outside.

COME TO SUNNY HAWAII a billboard opposite her flashed. AUSTRALIA AND THE PACIFIC! winked on the other side of the street. To Caroline the idea of running away and catching the next plane to Australia seemed wonderful, especially at that moment. She gazed at the billboards, picturing herself on a beach, lying in the sun with no schedule, no pressure, and no problems. If she had happened to find a few hundred dollars in her pocket, she would have headed for the airport, but as it was, the amount of cash she had was not even enough for another cup of hot chocolate. Even with slow sipping, she was near the bottom of the cup. She wondered if she would have to leave as soon as she finished. The thought of going out into the cold, wet evening again was enough to make her put the cup down with half an inch of chocolate left in the bottom.

Everybody else seemed to be in a hurry. People came into the cafe, gulped down a cup of coffee and left again. Buses screeched to the curb, sending a spray of cold water over the line of waiting passengers. Cars and taxis honked at

pedestrians who took too long crossing the
street. It was an unfriendly world, full of unfriendly people. Caroline looked down at her cup.
When she looked up again, a face was staring in
through the steamy glass, looking directly at her.
It was Chrissy, no doubt about it.

For a second Caroline wondered if Chrissy had
recognized her. She decided to ignore her cousin
in the hope that she would go away. But Chrissy
was already pushing open the door, bringing a
gust of cold air with her.

"What are you doing here?" she demanded
loudly. Several people turned around to look.

"Madame let us out early tonight," Caroline
said. "I needed a cup of hot chocolate before I
faced that hill home." She gave Chrissy what she
hoped was a bright, reassuring smile. Chrissy's
face remained stony.

"Bullshit!" she said. The people looked around
again.

Caroline looked at her suspiciously. "What do
you mean?"

"I mean you didn't go to your class tonight."
Chrissy said slowly.

"Yes, well you see, Madame decided that—"

"I went there, Caroline," Chrissy said. "It was
raining and I had my big umbrella and we were
downtown getting costume supplies, so I thought
I'd be a pal and walk you home. I spoke to your
Madame. . . ."

"Oh," Caroline said. "What did she say?"

"She said you had quit a week ago and she

hadn't seen you since."

"Oh," Caroline said again.

Chrissy continued to stare at her.

"Are you going to tell my folks?" Caroline asked at last.

Chrissy pulled up a stool and sat down beside her. "Why?" she asked.

"I couldn't take it anymore," Caroline said in a small voice. "I just couldn't take it. Being yelled at every night, working and working—for what? I don't even want to be a dancer, Chrissy."

"I didn't mean that," Chrissy said. "I meant why didn't you tell anyone?"

"I was sure Madame would call and tell Mom and Dad," Caroline said. "Then when she didn't, it got harder and harder to say anything."

"But why didn't you tell me?" Chrissy asked. "I thought we could tell each other anything."

"I knew what you'd say," Caroline replied. "You'd think I was being stupid, and you'd want me to tell my parents right away. I couldn't do that."

"You make it sound as if you have monsters for parents," Chrissy said. "Your parents are terrific people, Caroline. Do you think for one minute they'd force you to go on dancing if you didn't want to?"

Caroline shifted uneasily on her stool. "I didn't think that," she said, "but you saw what they were like—they were as excited as little kids about my competition. I didn't know how to tell them the truth without hurting them."

"How do you think they're going to feel now?" Chrissy asked quietly. "Don't you think you'll make them feel like two monsters who were so overpowering that their only child didn't dare tell them she was unhappy?"

Caroline sighed deeply. "I guess so. I've made a real mess of things, haven't I? A mess of my whole life . . ."

"Not too big a mess," Chrissy said. "You haven't committed a crime or gotten yourself thrown out of school. It's just a little mess, Caroline. One you can clear up in two seconds."

"But not without everybody being mad at me," Caroline said. She felt tears burning at the back of her eyes, and hoped she wouldn't start crying in the crowded coffee bar.

Chrissy leaned across and put her hand on her cousin's wet sleeve. "They'll feel sad, not mad, just the way I do," Chrissy said. "All I can think of is why you let us all go on believing that you were happy when you weren't. I had no idea, Caroline. I could tell you were uptight, but I thought that was just tension about the competition. Tracy and I both noticed that you didn't even want to be with us anymore, but we just thought you were really tense about getting the scholarship."

"I thought you didn't want me around," Caroline said. "I thought Tracy and you were best friends now and I didn't fit in anymore."

"You are a dummy," Chrissy said, shaking her head. "Of course we wanted you around. Just because Tracy and I are getting along well doesn't mean that we don't want you! You're not limited to one friend in this town, are you?"

Caroline managed a little laugh. "Everything's been going wrong for so long that I've been suspicious of everything and everyone."

"When did you start not liking your ballet classes?" Chrissy asked. "When we came to your performance you were in seventh heaven. You didn't hate them then, did you? Because if you did, you are a terrific actress."

"No, you're right. I didn't hate them then," Caroline said, "although I was beginning to hate the amount of time they took out of my life. I guess it was the musical that did it. . . ."

"The musical? I thought the musical was too amateur for you. That's what we all thought— that it wasn't good enough for a real dancer."

Caroline laughed uneasily. "That's what I wanted you to think. Everyone was pressuring me to drop out, and when you got the solo, it seemed like a good moment to quit. I didn't want anyone to know that I cared about it, or how important it was to me, or they'd all say I was only quitting because I was jealous."

"And were you?" Chrissy asked.

"More angry than jealous," Caroline answered. "I didn't not want you to get the solo. I just felt that I should have gotten it."

"You're a much better dancer, everyone knows that," Chrissy said. "But this solo isn't for your sort of dance. You'll see if you come back. Do you think you might?"

"Come back to the musical? I wish," Caroline said, "but they've already filled my place, haven't they?"

"They have an understudy, but she's so unreliable," Chrissy said. "She only shows up for practice when she feels like it. Greg has warned her a hundred times. I think he'd love to have you back."

"I'd like that," Caroline said. "I really miss that musical. It was being in it that reminded me that life should be fun. Nothing has been fun for me for the longest time."

"You've put too much pressure on yourself," Chrissy said.

"I know," Caroline admitted, "and look where it's gotten me—I tried to please everyone and ended up by pleasing nobody. I've deceived my parents, lost my boyfriend, and almost lost all my other friends, too."

"You'd never lose me," Chrissy said. "You're stuck with me until next summer, remember! Come on, let's go home. I'll help you tell your folks, if you like."

Caroline gave Chrissy a big smile. As she did, a tear escaped and trickled down her cheek. She brushed it away with embarrassment.

"Thanks, but I'll tell them myself," she said.

"Are you sure?" Chrissy asked. "I can call Tracy and tell her that I can't work on the costumes tonight, that something important just came up."

"I appreciate the offer Chrissy, but I'm the one

who made a mess of my life," Caroline admitted. "And I'm the one who's got to fix it."

The girls turned up their collars and went out, arm in arm under the big umbrella.

Chapter 11

Caroline's parents were sitting opposite each other in their big armchairs, watching TV as she slid silently into the living room. They didn't notice her come in—they were both staring intently at a National Geographic program about building wells in Africa. Caroline hesitated in the doorway, watching them.

This is like a scene out of a play, she thought. In her nervousness, she had to fight back a desire to giggle. Her father only needed a pipe to complete the scene, her mother knitting or needlepoint. The pipe and the knitting would gradually sink to their laps in bewilderment as she told them her terrible news. *Hey, wait a minute,* she reminded herself, *my news isn't that terrible. I'm not telling them that I'm wanted by the police, or pregnant, or about to marry a Soviet spy!*

In spite of her tension, she grinned to herself. At that moment her father looked up.

"Why, hello, Caroline," he said with a warm smile. "What are you doing creeping around?"

His smile was so friendly that Caroline's fear and tension instantly returned in full force. It was terrible news after all. When she lied to parents who trusted and loved her, it was terrible, however small the lie was. *Get this over with!* she commanded herself.

"Mom, Dad, I've got to talk to you," she began, her mind returning to the scene in the play. Why did she feel she was speaking lines already written for her? Any minute now her parents would say, "I don't understand, after all we've done for you!"

"Come and sit down," her father said, indicating the sofa between them. "You must be tired after all that dancing."

"That's what I wanted to talk about," Caroline went on.

"... and the Umboko tribe have an unusual ceremony!" the television set interrupted. Her father pressed the remote control to turn off the sound.

Caroline looked at her parents' expectant faces and felt guiltier than ever, but she knew she had to tell them—now.

"About ballet ..." she began again. On the silent screen men with feathered headdresses were turning round and round.

"Is it about the competition?" her mother asked gently.

Caroline nodded.

"You're worried about the competition?" her mother asked.

"That's it. You see . . ." She pulled herself up as another lie was about to slip out. "There won't be any competition," she said. The words came out in a rush. Her parents looked at her with interest, but not the horror she'd expected.

"I quit ballet school," she said. "I decided I don't want to be a ballet dancer."

She looked at the two people who were nodding earnestly, but not having hysterics.

"I can't believe it," she burst out. "I thought you two would just freak out when I told you. I thought you'd be so mad!"

"Why should we be mad about your choice for your future?" her father asked gently. "It's *your* future, after all. If you wanted to be a lion tamer or a mountain climber or even a punk rock star, we'd try to understand."

"You would?"

"What we'd like to know, Caroline," her mother interrupted, "is why you took so long to tell us."

"I tried to tell you the night that I quit," Caroline explained. "But you were so excited about the reception your boss was planning for me, you didn't give me a chance to explain. After that it got harder and harder until—" She broke off short, looking from one face to the other.

"Hey, wait a minute, you knew I'd quit ballet school?" she asked.

Her mother nodded. "Madame phoned the evening after you walked out."

"She phoned and you didn't say anything? You let me go on pretending?" Caroline demanded, swallowing hard.

"We figured it was up to you to tell us," her father said. "But we still can't understand why you went on pretending for so long."

"I thought you'd be mad," Caroline said. "I thought you'd make me go back."

Now it was her parents who exchanged a glance. "Caroline," her mother said in a hurt voice, "when have we ever forced you to do something?"

"You were so excited about this competition," Caroline said, looking past her parents to watch the plumed dancers still silently twirling. "You kept on telling me about your great hopes for my future. You had it all planned out—all the way up to *Swan Lake*. That's why I kept on so long, because you expected it of me. You wanted it so badly!"

"Oh, come on, Cara," her mother said, her voice shaking a little. "I was only excited for you, honeybun. Just the way any mother would be when her daughter is doing well—"

"No, Edith," her husband interrupted. "You did go a little overboard, you know. You talked the whole time as if Caroline were destined to be a great ballet star. I can understand how that could have sounded frightening for her if she'd already decided that ballet was not what she wanted for herself."

Caroline turned to look at her mother. For a long minute their eyes held each other's. "Is that how you felt?" her mother asked. "You felt trapped because of me?"

Caroline nodded.

"And you really hated ballet?"

"Oh, no," Caroline said. "I used to like ballet. I enjoyed dancing. I guess I stopped enjoying it when it got too serious—when everyone started assuming that I was going to be a professional some day. I hated having to be perfect in everything I did and be yelled at if my foot was half an inch too high. I saw that I'd never have the discipline to be a real dancer."

"So when did you decide that you wanted to stop?" her mother asked, almost as if she wanted to punish herself.

"I only realized I wanted to stop completely when I had this big fight with Madame," Caroline said. "Before that I knew I didn't like it, but I never thought I could walk out."

"What was this fight about?" her father asked. Caroline sensed a twinkle in his eyes, and suspected that he also felt that Madame needed someone to bring her down a notch.

"Didn't Madame tell you?"

"She said that you'd lost your temper and stormed out, but she expected you to be back. She was surprised when you didn't turn up, and wanted us to talk sense into you," her mother said gently.

"She must have known I wouldn't be back," Caroline said. "If she knew anything about people at all, she must have known how I felt. But that's right—she doesn't know about people. She doesn't care about any of her students. She pushed Tais over backward when Tais was still sick with the flu. She wasn't even sorry, Mom."

There was a long silence.

"And she was horrible to you, too?" her father asked at last.

Caroline shrugged her shoulders. "She yelled a lot."

Another silence.

"Cara, it was brave of you to walk out," her father said. "I'm sorry we put you through a lot of anguish. I want you to know that you can always come to us. Never be scared of telling us things, however bad they might seem. Promise me?"

Caroline got up and walked over to his chair. "Okay, Dad," she said. "I'll remember that. I'm sorry I didn't tell you sooner."

Her father got up and wrapped her in a big bear hug. "No, we're sorry, honey. We're sorry we weren't more sensitive to your feelings. It wasn't fair on you to feel that you were trapped into doing something you hated. From now on you just do fun things, right?" Caroline felt his hug almost crushing her ribs.

"Right, Dad," she said, half laughing through shining tears.

Over his shoulder she looked across at her mother. Mrs. Kirby still sat in the big armchair, looking down at her hands. A terrifying thought caused Caroline's tension to return. *Mom's still mad at me. She can't come out and say it, because she knows Dad would never agree with her, but she can't forgive me for quitting.*

She pushed herself free from her father's arms. "I'm feeling tired and hungry. Maybe I'll just take some soup to my room tonight. Chrissy's out, and I'll get an early night."

Caroline didn't look back at her parents, and nobody spoke. She noticed that her mother did not get up and follow her into the kitchen to prepare her meal the way she usually did. Caroline started to heat up the soup, hoping that the warm food would get rid of the sick feeling in her stomach. *I guess nothing is simple in this life,* she thought bleakly. *Just when you think everything is sorted out, you realize that there are more complications. . . .*

She only managed to eat half a bowl of soup before crawling into bed.

It shouldn't matter to me what she thinks, Caroline kept telling herself. *Of course she's disappointed, because she had such high hopes for me. But I'm the only person who can really decide my future. She must realize that. Even if she's mad at me now, she'll understand soon.*

But the pep talk did not make her feel much better. She was curled into a tight little ball when her door opened quietly. She didn't open her eyes. She wasn't in a mood to talk to Chrissy.

Then someone sat down gently on her bed. "Caroline?" her mother's voice asked. "Are you asleep?"

Caroline uncurled, and opened her eyes.

"Caroline, I had to talk to you before you go to sleep," her mother said. "I've been feeling so bad all evening. I didn't know what to say before."

Caroline lifted her head on the pillow so that she could look at her mother. The hall light threw a strip of brightness across her bed. Her mother sat looking down at her hands, much as she had earlier.

"I thought you might still be mad at me," Caroline said hesitantly.

Her mother looked up, amazed. "Why should I be mad at you, honeybun? You haven't done anything wrong."

"I quit ballet. You wanted me to be a ballerina."

There was a silence. Then her mother said uneasily, "I couldn't say what I felt before because I was feeling so mad at *me*—that I put you through so much unhappiness. I was really self-ish, Caroline—please forgive me."

Caroline heaved a huge sigh of relief. "Oh, Mom, that's okay. It's only natural that you encourage me to succeed. All parents do that—look at Little League fathers!"

Her mother laughed uncomfortably. "Was I as bad as a Little League father?" Before Caroline could reply, she said, "No, don't answer that. I guess I was. I've been going over some of the things I said to you, and I can't believe myself. I was making all these plans—I was even talking about moving to New York, and I never once asked you—"

"I tried to tell you, several times—" Caroline began.

"Of course you did, honeybun, I know that now," her mother went on. "I realize how many times you tried to let me know and I just walked all over your feelings. I was the worst kind of pushy mother."

Caroline smiled. "No, not the worst kind," she said. "You didn't try to do my auditions for me, or even sit in at my classes. Some mothers do that."

Her mother smiled suddenly, too, as if a load had been lifted from her shoulders. "Thank heavens for that. No, I've never auditioned for you. It wouldn't have helped you much if I had. I think that was why I wanted this so much for you. I would have loved to be a ballerina, but out where we lived in Iowa, there was no question of ballet lessons. Nobody was prepared to drive me fifty miles to the nearest town. I guess I transferred all my frustrated ambition to you."

Caroline reached out and covered her mother's hand with her own. "I'm sorry I couldn't have been a ballerina for you, Mom."

Her mother looked down at Caroline and gently smoothed the hair back from her forehead. "You mustn't ever be anything to please anybody else, ever," she said firmly. "Your life is your own, and if I even start to interfere again, you tell me about it right away! I can't promise I'll never do it, but I'll try, Cara—and I'll try to be more of a friend who has time to listen."

Caroline bit her lip as she squeezed her mother's hand. "Thanks, Mom," she said.

That night she slept soundly and without nightmares for the first time in weeks.

Chapter 12

Caroline was torn in two about coming back to the musical and needed a lot of urging from Chrissy before she finally agreed to ask Greg about it.

"What's wrong, Caroline?" Chrissy asked her. "I thought you loved the musical before and you hated to give it up. Don't you want to come back anymore?"

"Part of me does," Caroline answered. "Every-time I think of going to rehearsals with all those people again and doing those dances, I feel really excited, but . . ."

"But?" Chrissy asked.

"I'm going to look like a failure, Chrissy," Caroline said with a sigh. "As soon as they see me back at rehearsals, they're all going to know that I flunked the big dance contest. They'll know I wasn't such a hotshot ballerina after all."

"So just tell them the truth," Chrissy said, shaking her head as if she sometimes found Caroline hard to understand. "Tell them that you didn't want that pressure anymore and you decided that ballet wasn't for you. What's there to be ashamed of? Everyone at school is going to change their minds about career plans a hundred times. That's all you are doing—that's not failure!"

Caroline looked across at her hopefully. "When you put it like that. . ." she said.

"How else is there to put it?" Chrissy asked. "Obviously only a dummy would walk in and say 'Guess what folks, I got flung out of ballet school because I wasn't good enough, so I came back here.'"

Caroline laughed. "That's not even true," she said. "I could have been good enough. I just didn't want it."

"So tell them that," Chrissy said. "What you've needed for the past ten years is not lessons in step of the cat, but lessons in step of the confidence. I know getting that solo has done wonders for my confidence here! I used to be a really confident person, then everything was turned upside down for me when I came here, but now I'm definitely back on my feet again!"

"I'm glad, Chrissy," Caroline said.

"And you won't mind too much about me dancing that solo?" Chrissy asked. "It's really not your sort of dance—there's no step of the cats in it."

Caroline laughed easily. "Of course I won't mind. Just don't knock over any lamps, okay?"

"That's terrific, then," Chrissy exclaimed. "Let's go talk to Greg right now!"

Caroline could see from Greg's face that he was delighted to have her back, and that made her feel good.

"I'm going to need you around to cope with the little problems that are starting to crop up," he said.

"There are problems with the routines?" Caroline asked in surprise.

"More attitudes than routines," Greg said with a quick glance around the room.

Caroline thought she understood. Probably the understudy who never showed up had made everybody else slack off. Caroline knew it only took one person to spoil the atmosphere. "I'll help any way I can," she said.

He beamed down at her. "That's my girl," he said, and smiled in a way that melted her down to her toes.

Nobody has smiled at me like that since Alex, she thought, then stopped short before she could finish the sentence. Alex was still too painful to think about. Now that she had more time and less problems, she was acutely aware that he had gone, and the gap he'd left in her life was still a big, empty void that couldn't be filled.

If only there were a way to get him back

again—to tell him how much I miss him and want him back. I know it would be different this time, Caroline thought. But Alex had been the only real boyfriend she'd ever had, and she hadn't the slightest idea how to bring him back. It had seemed like a miracle that Alex even noticed her in the first place. Now she couldn't imagine ever meeting another boy who might make her feel as wonderful as Alex had.

Caroline tried not to think about Alex. She tried not to catch glimpses of him in the halls between classes. In fact she had become skilled in switching off the beginning of Alex-thoughts by the time she arrived at rehearsal with Chrissy. But, of course, the first person she saw as she entered the auditorium was Jan.

Caroline's stomach constricted into that old familiar knot as Chrissy pulled her toward the front of the room. Jan was laughing as she told a joke. Her peacock-blue leotard accented her copper-colored hair and her blue-green eyes. Caroline hadn't remembered that she was quite that pretty. Jan broke off telling the story as she saw Caroline and Chrissy come into the hall.

"Look who's here, everyone," Chrissy yelled out, making Caroline turn scarlet-cheeked with embarrassment. "Caroline's decided she'd rather dance with us than dance in New York!"

The faces that turned toward Caroline were all friendly, and the girls from the chorus crowded around her.

"Chrissy told us you had a big fight with your ballet teacher when she pushed some girl over and broke her ankle!" Nancy said, looking at Caroline with admiration mixed with concern. "I'm real sorry you had to stop your training like that. Do you think you'll find another ballet school?"

Caroline felt grateful to Chrissy for making up a story about her, so she didn't contradict her cousin's version. Instead she shook her head and said, "I don't think I want to be a professional dancer anymore. I'll stick to things like high school musicals."

"Well, no fancy stuff, okay?" Nancy asked. "I still can't get my kicks as high as my shoulder. I don't want you to show us all up!"

"I wouldn't do that," Caroline said. "It will be a relief for me to be one of a chorus and not to have someone criticizing every move I make."

"I know what you mean," one of the other girls chimed in. "I went to that ballet school for a while. When the teacher hit my leg with her stick, that was enough for me. You must be really tough to stick it out for so long."

Surrounded by their warmth and praise, Caroline made her way up onto the stage, where Greg appeared from the lighting booth. He gave Caroline a wink that made her feel warm all over. "Good to see you, Cara," he said. "Now we'll get some work done around here again. Caroline knows what real work is. If I let her run my rehearsals, she'll make you do the same exercise until you drop."

The others shot Caroline nervous glances. Caroline gave an equally nervous glance at Greg. He laughed out loud. "That's got you on your toes, hasn't it? Okay, act three, scene one. Let's go through the farmer and cowman number." He turned to Caroline. "Go over with Jan in that corner, Cara—she'll show you what we were doing."

Caroline looked up to see Jan staring at her across the stage, and wondered if Jan felt as embarrassed as she did. She walked slowly into position beside Alex's new girlfriend.

"Hi," Jan said, her lips twitching in a smile.

"Hi."

They both looked down, then glanced up at each other again. Caroline was thinking desperately of something to say.

Then Jan said, "I heard you had to drop out of your ballet?"

"I didn't have to. I wanted to," Caroline mumbled.

"I'm sorry it didn't work out," Jan whispered as Greg began giving the dancers instructions.

"It's okay. I'm glad about it," Caroline said.

"And I'm glad you're back with us," Jan said, a little more easily now. "We sure need someone to get us through these numbers. Greg's tearing his hair out over the finale. None of us knows our right from our left."

She grinned shyly at Caroline. The grin was so obviously a plea for acceptance that Caroline had to smile back. *I can't be mad at her,* she thought in amazement. *She's a nice person. It's not her fault that my boyfriend liked her better.* . . .

The music started up. "Quick, what comes first?" Caroline whispered to Jan.

"It's the boys first," Jan whispered back. "Then our budding star does her solo."

"You mean Chrissy?" Caroline asked in amazement.

Jan nodded. "Oh, don't get me wrong," she whispered. "Chrissy's a nice girl, and I know she's your cousin, but she's starting to act like a big shot around here."

"Chrissy is?" Caroline asked. "My cousin Chrissy?"

"That's right."

"I can't believe it!" Caroline exclaimed.

"Just watch for a few minutes. You'll see for yourself," Jan said, staring at Chrissy across the stage.

Caroline also turned her gaze on Chrissy. *Surely Jan must be mistaken, or even jealous?* she thought. Caroline had seen no hint of success going to Chrissy's head. She hadn't been acting like a big-shot star around the house—she hadn't made any outrageous demands or boastful comments—and so far during rehearsal Chrissy had been lively, of course, but no more than usual.

Jan's got to be jealous because Chrissy is doing the solo, Caroline thought, *or she's trying to stir up trouble between Chrissy and me.*

Chrissy's music started and she began to dance.

Caroline saw instantly what Chrissy had meant
when she said it was not Caroline's sort of dance.
It was a real hillbilly type of number with a lot of
foot-stomping and strutting. Greg had exagger-
ated all the moves to make it into a comedy
number, and Chrissy did it perfectly. As she
danced she flirted with one man after another
around the room, always moving away just in
time with a shrug of her shoulder or a swish of
her petticoats. As Caroline watched her cousin,
she knew that Greg had chosen well. The result
was a fun number in which Chrissy's personality
really shone through. When she finished, Caroline felt the urge to applaud.

"That was great, Chrissy," Greg said. "Now let's
go right into the square dance."

"Before we do that, Greg, I want to bring
something up," Chrissy said loudly. "About the
way those couples hold each other around the
waist. It's wrong—that's not the way it's really
done."

"It's a stage dance, not the real thing, Chrissy,"
Greg said calmly. "We have them hold around the
waist because it looks best."

"Oh, and another thing," Chrissy added, turning to glance at the half-painted backdrop behind
them. "What month of the year are we supposed
to be in?"

"How would I know?" Greg no longer sounded
calm.

"Because we've got something on that scenery
that needs to be changed," Chrissy continued. "If

the corn is as high as an elephant's eye, then it must be the middle of summer, so how can that dogwood tree be in bloom?"

"It's just scenery, Chrissy—to look good," Greg said. "We needed a bit of color behind the house."

"But it's not right, Greg," Chrissy insisted. "I should know. I live in a house like that and we have a dogwood tree in the front yard."

"It doesn't have to be right—it's representational," Greg said. "Now, for Pete's sake let's get on with the square dance number."

Caroline watched as Chrissy reluctantly stepped aside. She had to admit that Jan had been right—Chrissy was really being a pain.

After that Caroline had to concentrate on picking up the square dance steps, and was pleased when Greg switched the positions around so that her couple was out in the front. It was also a wonderful experience not to be yelled at when she didn't get things right immediately. Once the couples collided when crossing the floor diagonally, and Greg laughed as much as anyone did. It seemed that only one thing was bugging him about this show, and that was Chrissy.

After the rehearsal Greg called Caroline aside.

"Was I okay?" Caroline asked nervously, wondering what the talk was going to be about.

"You were terrific," he said, giving her shoulder a squeeze. "You picked it up so quickly, and you're a joy to watch. It wasn't about you I wanted to talk. . . ."

"About Chrissy, huh?" Caroline asked, looking over her shoulder at her cousin's back disappearing down the auditorium.

Greg nodded. "You saw her today?"

"I couldn't believe it," Caroline said. "That's just not like her to want to throw her weight around."

"Well, she'd doing it with monotonous regularity," Greg said bitterly. "We have to stop because the baskets are not right for picking apples or the scarecrow isn't correct for corn or you don't put cows behind that sort of fence. She even wanted us to have a live baby pig on stage!" He put his hand up and ran it through his black curls. "My God, Caroline, she's trying to turn this into *Farmer's Weekly*! It's very distracting to everyone else, too. It breaks their concentration."

"I can see that," Caroline said.

"So talk to her, will you?" Greg asked. "Tell her to knock it off or she's out of the play. I tried talking to her once, but she launched into a lecture on agriculture in the midwest. I'm scared if I say anything else I'll lose my temper, and I hate doing that. Maybe she'd listen to you?"

"I'll try," Caroline said. "I don't know why she's acting so strangely. Maybe she doesn't realize how much she's bugging everyone. I'll talk to her this evening, Greg."

Greg looked down at her with dark, warm eyes. "You are a lifesaver, Caroline—or rather, you're going to save my sanity! If I hear one more thing about dogwoods or hog food, I'll throw myself in the bay screaming!"

Caroline laughed. "Don't do that," she said.

Greg put his hands on both her shoulders and held her firmly for a moment. "Not if you stick around, I won't," he whispered, then released her, bounding up onto the stage with his long, agile legs.

Caroline hurried after Chrissy, her head buzzing in confusion and her heart beating rapidly.

Chapter 19

Chapter 13

Caroline didn't say anything to Chrissy on the way home about her behavior at rehearsal. Tracy was walking with them, and Caroline didn't want to embarrass her cousin. Besides, Caroline's mind was still in a muddle at the memory of Greg's hands on her shoulders and his eyes smiling down into hers.

You're imagining things, she told herself severely, letting her attention wander from the girls' discussion about costumes. *Greg is the director of the play. He's a college student—how could he possibly be interested in a little high school girl? He's friendly like that to all the girls in his cast, so don't go falling madly in love with him just because he has the cutest brown eyes and the most wonderful smile—*

Caroline's thought was interrupted when something else occurred to her. Just that afternoon she'd been thinking that she would never get over Alex and never fall in love again. Now her heart was already beating fast at the thought of Greg! Even if he was out of her league, it was nice to know that life hadn't ended with Alex. There was still a lot to look forward to!

She broke into a jog to catch up with Chrissy and Tracy, and they talked about costumes all the way home. It wasn't until Tracy had gone home and the girls were loading the dinner plates into the dishwasher that Caroline found herself alone with Chrissy.

"So are you glad I made you come back to the play?" Chrissy asked, beaming at Caroline.

"Of course I am," Caroline said, scrubbing hard at the big saucepan that had held the Chinese noodles. "You know I never wanted to leave in the first place."

"Greg's obviously glad you're back," Chrissy said, giving Caroline a knowing grin. "If he weren't so much older—"

"Well, he is," Caroline replied hastily. "He was just making me feel welcome to be back."

"Is that what he was doing?" Chrissy said with a broad grin. "Maybe I should go away and be welcomed back then."

Caroline felt her cheeks turning pink. "Come on, Chrissy," she said. "You know that Greg's just a warm and friendly person. He likes to make his cast feel relaxed."

"I haven't noticed him being too warm or friendly toward the rest of us recently," Chrissy said, stacking the plates into the bottom rack as she spoke. "In fact he's been decidedly cold, I'd say."

Caroline took a deep breath. "Maybe that's because of you, Chrissy," she said quietly.

Chrissy looked up from the dishwasher in amazement. "Me? What on earth do you mean?"

"I mean the way you've been behaving."

"I don't get you! I've been behaving perfectly normally."

"For a prima donna, yes!" Caroline said. "I saw you today, Chrissy. Everybody has noticed it."

"Noticed what, for heaven's sake?" Chrissy asked, eyeing Caroline suspiciously.

"The way you throw your weight around, like you're the star of the play," Caroline said, wincing with embarrassment at the words.

Chrissy's mouth hung open with astonishment. "Me?" she asked in a high-pitched squeak. "Me, act like the star? You've got to be joking. When have I ever acted like the star?"

Caroline looked at her steadily. "Oh, Greg, the dogwood is wrong. The square dance is wrong," she mimicked. "Greg told me you were driving him up the wall, criticizing all the time."

Chrissy's mouth was still wide open as a bright crimson flush rose in her cheeks. "He said I was criticizing all the time?"

"Well, aren't you?" Caroline asked.

Chrissy stopped to think for a moment, putting

her hand to her flaming cheek. "Caroline, I only mention when they've got something wrong. I didn't realize they'd think I was throwing my weight around. It's just that I know how things really are on a farm, and none of them do."

"But it's a stage farm, Chrissy. It doesn't matter whether it's right or wrong."

"It does to me," Chrissy said in a small voice. "It matters a lot to me."

"Mama Mia, Chrissy—it's only a play," Caroline said gently.

Chrissy turned away and began furiously stacking silverware in the dishwasher. "How would you feel if you were in a play about San Francisco and they painted the Golden Gate the wrong color and they had cable cars making the wrong noise?" she asked. "I bet you'd tell them they'd got it wrong."

Caroline considered the notion. "I probably would," she said.

"Well, they keep on getting things wrong in the play—things that are part of my home and my life, and I can't keep quiet about them," Chrissy said. "You don't understand how I feel about this. . . ."

Caroline put a hand on her cousin's shoulder. "I think I do, Chrissy," she said.

Chrissy made a noise that sounded dangerously like a sob. "It's more than that, Cara," she said. "It's because I'm homesick, you see. When we first started out in this play and it was all about a farm, I thought it would be great and would stop me from feeling homesick. But it's been just the opposite. Every time I'm up on that stage with fake corn and a fake barn, it reminds me how far away home really is. I have to keep pointing out what's wrong to remind myself of what home is really like."

She put her soapy hands up to her cheeks and brushed away tears, leaving two patches of froth in their place. Caroline looked at Chrissy's sad face. "Are you very homesick, Chrissy?" she asked. "You've been getting along so well, I didn't think you missed your family so much anymore."

"I do," Chrissy said. "In a way I miss them even more right now. I've been getting more and more homesick since fall started. I keep thinking of all the things we'd be doing around the farm and how I'm not there to help with them this year."

"It won't be long until Christmas," Caroline said gently. "Then you get to go home and visit. You can put up a calendar and count off the days!"

Chrissy nodded. "It's Thanksgiving I'm thinking of," she said. "I was talking to your mom about your plans for Thanksgiving, and she said you didn't bother with a turkey for only three of you and you usually went out to eat instead. I couldn't help thinking about our Thanksgiving at home. . . . Oh, Cara, it's the best time of year for me."

"Really?" Caroline asked, trying to picture what Thanksgiving would be like in Iowa.

Chrissy's eyes grew wistful. "We have the big-

gest turkey you can imagine. It only just fits into
the old wood-burning oven that we use for
special holidays. Grandma Madden comes, and
all the folks from King City way—Cousin Dutch
and the kids. Sometimes there's twenty of us
around the table and the kids have to sit at the
card table covered with a piece of plywood down
at one end, but nobody minds being squashed.
Everyone brings something—you know, the old
tradition of seven sweets and seven sours, and
my Dad keeps carving and carving." She paused
and laughed. "It's so noisy with everyone talking
and laughing at the same time, and there's a big
fire crackling in the hearth and snowflakes fluttering outside . . . it's just—it's very special."

Caroline nodded with understanding. "It
sounds very special," she said. "Chrissy I've got
an idea—why don't you call your folks and ask if
you can come home for Thanksgiving? I don't
know how much it costs, but maybe it's not too
much. It's worth a try."

"Maybe," Chrissy said hesitantly. "I have a little
money saved. I could use that toward the ticket."
She turned to Caroline, her face suddenly alive
and her eyes shining. "Do you think I could call
them tonight and ask?"

"I'm sure my parents wouldn't mind," Caroline
said. "Remember they told you that you could
phone home whenever you wanted?"

"You make me sound like E.T.," Chrissy said
with a watery smile. "And I have to confess that
sometimes I feel like E.T.—there have been times

when everything seems so strange that I begin to wonder if I'm on another planet."

"Oh, come on Chrissy," Caroline said with a giggle. "We're strange in San Francisco, I know that, but not another planet!"

Chrissy looked suddenly serious. "If you ever come to Iowa and stay with my family, you'll see how different things are in Iowa compared to here. I've had to learn a whole new set of rules to live by, and it wears me out, Cara, because I can never really relax. I always have to be alert so that I don't make a fool of myself. Maybe that's why I'm extra homesick right now—I'm just plain tired. I need a good sleep in my own bed and my mother's good food to fatten me up."

"Anyone would think we starved you here," Caroline said with amusement.

"Oh, don't think I'm criticizing," Chrissy said hastily. "You feed me plenty, but there's nothing like the food you grow up with, is there? You wait until you taste my mother's homemade pies. . . ."

"I have a horrible feeling I'd put on a hundred pounds overnight," Caroline said. Then a wonderful truth dawned on her. "Chrissy, do you realize it doesn't matter if I gain weight anymore, because I'm not in ballet! It just fully hit me that I'm not in ballet!" She danced around the room, waving the sponge in her hand. "I'm free! I'm free! I can get as fat as I like! I can watch TV at night! I can go to the movies—"

"Hey, watch where you are shaking that water!" Chrissy interrupted, grabbing Caroline's hand. "You've soaked me and you've soaked the cabinets!" She shook her head seriously. "I think I'd better go home for Thanksgiving, for your sanity. When I first got here you were quiet and reserved and shy. Now you're dancing around yelling, and rapidly in danger of turning into me!"

"That wouldn't be half bad," Caroline said, still laughing. "I'd love to be friendly and outgoing like you, to be able to come right out and say what I feel. If only I hadn't clammed up on how much my ballet classes were upsetting me, I'd have saved myself a whole lot of worry, and I'd probably still have Alex. . . ."

Chrissy stopped laughing. She took the sponge and began wiping off the kitchen counter. "Does it still hurt a lot?" she asked. Then she answered for herself. "Dumb question, of course it hurts a lot. If I lost Ben to another girl, it would hurt me, I know."

"It's not quite as bad now," Caroline said. "At first I was numb, and I thought I'd never fall in love again as long as I live. But do you know what, Chrissy?" she asked, then continued before her cousin could answer. "Today I noticed that Greg made my heart beat faster when he put his hands on my shoulders, so perhaps there is hope for me after all!"

"Just don't fall in love too heavily with Greg," Chrissy warned. "He's much too old for you, and I bet a cute guy like that has a girlfriend lurking around someplace. Besides, can you imagine how your parents would flip if you told them you were dating a guy who's twenty-one?"

Caroline laughed, "Oh, don't worry about me," she said. "I'm being realistic, but it is a great feeling to have a guy like Greg pay attention to me. It makes me hope that I won't have to go through the rest of my life without a boyfriend."

"As if you would," Chrissy said. "You'll have guys lined up waiting, just as soon as you learn to come out of your shell and not be so shy."

"Minor point," Caroline said seriously. "The way I'm going, I can see myself sixty-five years old and still shy."

"I don't think so, Cara. I mean, you stood up to that creepy old Madame, and that takes guts," Chrissy reminded her.

"Yeah," Caroline agreed, a smile slowly lighting up her face." That's a pretty good start, isn't it?"

"It sure is," Chrissy said. "Hey, Cara—do you think I could go phone my folks right now? Otherwise it will be too late because of the time difference."

"Of course you can," Caroline said. "Go right ahead. Use the phone in my parents' bedroom if you want privacy."

"Oh, wow," Chrissy yelled, bounding toward the door. "I can't wait. I've got so much to tell them . . . I'm so excited. . . ."

Caroline watched her go. *So Chrissy's back to her usual loud, bouncy self*, she thought. Then she realized that she hadn't paid any attention to the fact that Chrissy had been extraordinarily quiet during the past few weeks. Poor Chrissy had been feeling homesick and had nobody to tell about it—*because I've been wrapped up in my own problems and never noticed,* Caroline thought.

When everything was going wrong at ballet and then with Alex, she'd never stopped to think that other people might have problems, too. She had shut herself into a private world of her own misery. Now, for the first time, she realized fully how much hurt she could have saved herself if she'd talked about her worries to Chrissy. Maybe then Chrissy would have confided her own homesickness, and each of their burdens would have been easier to bear.

I'm going to make a big effort never to shut myself away with my problems again, Caroline vowed.

Chapter 14

Caroline finished cleaning the kitchen and went to her bedroom to begin her homework. She could hear the drone of Chrissy's voice through the bedroom door. *I bet her folks will be thrilled to get a call from her,* she thought. Chrissy had never dared call home before. She'd said that hearing the sound of her family's voices would just make her homesick. Now Chrissy's voice droned on and on, sometimes rising in pitch, followed by moments of silence.

I bet they'll want her to come home for Thanksgiving, Caroline thought as she took out her chemistry book and opened it. *I bet they've been missing her as much as she's been missing them. It will be so nice for her to be back with a big family again. It must seem so quiet and dull here for her, and I know she wouldn't like our Thanks-*

*giving. Hers sounded like fun—I'd love to try
living with a big family, sitting at a table with all
those people. . . .*

Her thoughts were interrupted as she heard
Chrissy hang up the phone and make her way
down the hall.

"Well?" Caroline asked excitedly. "What did
they say? Did they think it was a great—" She
broke off in mid sentence as Chrissy's face appeared around the door. "Chrissy, what's the
matter? Is something wrong?" she asked, leaping
up from her chair.

"Oh, Cara," Chrissy said, and threw herself
down on her bed and burst into tears.

"Chrissy, what is it?" Caroline asked nervously.
"Please don't cry like that. Tell me what's happened. Did they say you couldn't come home?"

"Oh, Cara, it's terrible," Chrissy sobbed at last.
"They didn't want to tell me about it before,
because they didn't want to worry me."

She broke into more loud sobs, burying her
face in her pillow, her whole body wracked with
shudders. Caroline stood beside her cousin, feeling scared and sick. She'd never seen anyone cry
like that, and coming from Chrissy, it was especially alarming. Chrissy's news must have been
really terrible. . . .

"Chrissy, what is it?" she asked again. "Is it
someone in your family?"

"It's . . .it's . . . the barn," Chrissy managed to
gulp out at last.

"The barn?" Caroline had an absurd desire to

laugh. "The barn?" she asked again.

Chrissy lifted her head from the pillow enough to stare at Caroline through reddened eyes. "A tornado touched down and took the barn away," she said.

"But that's not the worst thing in the world," Caroline said softly. "I was expecting something really terrible, like something had happened to one of your brothers."

"One of my brothers wouldn't make me cry as much as the barn," Chrissy said, with a small attempt at a laugh.

"But surely you have insurance and that will pay?" Caroline asked. "They do pay up for tornadoes, don't they?"

Chrissy shook her head slowly. "You don't understand how bad it is, Caroline," she said.

"Why don't you tell me about it." Caroline sank to the edge of the bed beside Chrissy.

"It was a very old barn, you see. My grandfather built it and it really needed replacing, but Dad always said it would stand a few more years." Chrissy sniffled, then went on. "Well, now it's gone and the insurance people say they're not paying up because it was about to collapse anyway. Well, we need a new barn for winter. We'd lose this year's calves and our hay would be ruined without a barn. Dad's trying to get a loan to pay for some of it, but in the meantime he's had to use some of our savings for a down payment. There's no money for me to come home, Cara."

Caroline touched Chrissy's back gently. "Chrissy, I'm so sorry," she said. "I know how much you wanted to be with your family for Thanksgiving. But we all love you here, you know."

Chrissy nodded. "I know," she said, "but it's even worse than that, Cara. I don't think I can go home for Christmas either."

"Did your parents say that?" Caroline asked in surprise.

"Of course not," Chrissy said. "They'd never say that they didn't want to see me. I told them that I thought I wanted to stay on here because it was hardly worth going home for such a short time."

Caroline stared at Chrissy with growing admiration.

"They could use that money, you see," Chrissy went on. "I don't want to give them an extra worry, and the fare home is not cheap around holiday times."

It occurred to Caroline that she had never thought much about her parents' finances. When she wanted something, like costumes for a ballet, all she had to do was ask. Now she wondered if those costumes or any of the other luxuries she'd enjoyed had ever caused her parents to worry about money. Caroline winced as she recalled begging her parents to let her go to Europe this past summer. She could almost feel herself growing up, as if she had stepped out of the protected cocoon of childhood and was suddenly aware of the real world. She couldn't help feeling ashamed that Chrissy had automatically put her family before something she wanted so much, while she had always thought of herself first.

"You're a very nice person, you know that?" Caroline told her cousin. "I think your parents are lucky to have a daughter like you. And we'll have a great Christmas here. We'll go skiing, maybe. Have you ever skied?"

"No, never . . . well, at least not down a hill," Chrissy said, and managed a little grin.

The next day Caroline told her mother about Chrissy's call home. "I'd really like to do something special for her on Thanksgiving," she said.

"Such as what?" her mother asked. "Take her on a trip somewhere?"

Caroline wrinkled her forehead. "No, I don't think so. I'd like to give her a Thanksgiving like the ones she gets at home."

Her mother laughed. "Are you planning to invite half of San Francisco?" she asked. "Because as I remember Thanksgivings back in Iowa, there was always half of Danbury around the table."

"I thought maybe we could invite Tracy and her family. There's just Tracy and her parents and her little sister, and I don't think they're going all the way to Hawaii to visit their relatives. And I'll invite my friend Tais from ballet school. We could have a really big turkey, Mom, and all the things you remember—those seven sweets and seven sours, whatever they are, and a big fire. . . ."

Her mother laughed. "All right. Fine with me, but you're in charge. I have an important exhibit coming up right after the Thanksgiving weekend, so I'll be super-busy."

"I don't mind. I'll do it," Caroline said. "It will be fun surprising Chrissy, just the way she surprised me with that party. Don't say a word about it, okay?"

"My lips are sealed," her mother said, laughing. "Only perhaps you'd better keep it a secret from your father—you know how absentminded he can be. He's likely to blurt it out at the dinner table."

"Good idea, we won't tell him," Caroline said. "It will be nice for him to have a surprise, too."

In the days before Thanksgiving Caroline threw herself into the preparations with enthusiasm. She found it was fun doing something nice for someone else. As an only child Caroline had always gotten all the attention—especially on holidays. But now she felt a warm glow as she imagined Chrissy's face when she saw the Thanksgiving dinner.

Caroline had talked to Tracy, and her family had gladly accepted the invitation. Tais, however, had to decline, since she would be spending the holiday in Nevada with her family, before coming back to San Francisco for extra rehearsals before the competition.

Caroline was extra glad now that she had no more ballet classes. That left her with plenty of time to slip down to the library and pore through the cookbook section to get recipes for some of the seven sweets and seven sours—dishes such as cranberry sauce, candied yams, pickled cabbage, and German chocolate cake. Some of the items seemed too complicated for her to cook on her own, so she ended up buying them ready-made at the grocery store. She even bought two pumpkin pies at a really fancy bakery.

On Thanksgiving day all Caroline had to do was stuff the turkey and prepare the vegetables. The recipes all looked simple enough, even, thank heavens, the candied yams, which she'd never even eaten before. She and her mother had come up with a good plan to get Chrissy out of the house. Caroline had begged her father to take her and Chrissy to a Thanksgiving fair being held across the bay. Then, on Thanksgiving morning, she claimed to have woken with a bad cold.

"Why don't you and Chrissy go to the fair without me?" she asked. "No sense in all of us having a boring Thanksgiving."

"Good idea," her father had agreed. "Then maybe you'll feel well enough to eat out somewhere tonight. What do you think of Thai food? That should be good for colds and sore throats."

Caroline caught the wistful look in Chrissy's eyes as they discussed eating Thanksgiving dinner at a Thai restaurant. Again the warmth crept up inside her until she was glowing all over.

"I must say you look a bit feverish," her father

said, eyeing her critically. "Your eyes are too bright. Go back to bed for the day."

So Chrissy and her father had departed, and Caroline got to work. To Caroline's relief, her mother came home from the gallery around noon to lend a hand. There was no way Caroline could have finished all the preparations by herself.

"Now I know why they have big families in the country," she said, pushing her hair back from her sweaty face as she leaned over to baste the turkey. "They need that many people to do the cooking, the way they like to eat."

Her mother chuckled and went on peeling potatoes. "When we were young, Chrissy's mother and I had to help with the cooking every day," she said. "To me it was a big chore, and I couldn't wait to get away from home and not cook anymore. I think that's why we eat out so much here. I never did like cooking."

"Oh, I think it's fun," Caroline said.

"Splendid. We'll let you cook for us from now on," her mother said as she took a tray of potatoes across to the oven. "We'll have home-made bread and pies every day and all get as fat as pigs."

"Well, of course, I don't know how I'd feel about it every day," Caroline said hastily. "I meant it's fun once in a while. Especially when it's a surprise for someone else. I feel like I'm in *Little House on the Prairie.*"

"I've just had a good idea," her mother said.

"Why don't you put on your play costume with all the petticoats? That will do wonders to create atmosphere."

"When I've finished cooking," Caroline agreed. "I get splattered every time I try and baste this thing. I swear it waits for me to open the oven door then spits me right in the eye!"

They had barely finished laying the table and putting another log on the fire when the Wongs arrived.

"I'm so glad you asked us," Tracy whispered to Caroline. "We have the most boring Thanksgiving at home. We never have a turkey because it's just the four of us, and we all hate turkey leftovers. We generally go out for Chinese food."

"So do we," Caroline exclaimed. "We should have found this out years ago, then at least we could have gone to the same restaurant."

Tracy looked at her. "Funny how long we've known each other, yet we don't know so many things," she said. "When will Chrissy be back?"

"Mom told my dad to be back at five," Caroline said. "We didn't dare tell him about the surprise dinner—he'd probably forget and blab about it. I just hope he doesn't get involved in something at the fair and lose track of time."

But almost on the stoke of five the front door opened.

"Anyone home? We're back," Caroline's father called. "I had to stop Chrissy spending all her money on the hand-crafted jewelry at the fair."

"And I had to stop him spending all his money

on homemade candies," Chrissy called out. It was clear they'd had a good day. They pushed open the door to the living room and stood speechless in the doorway. The fire burned brightly in the hearth, illuminating the table laden with platters of food and gleaming silverware. In the center was a big decoration of pinecones, wheat, and berries, created by Caroline's mother. Caroline had dimmed the lights and scattered candles about the room which cast soft shadows. Chrissy's wide-eyed face turned from the table to the Wongs to her aunt and cousin.

"I don't think I've ever seen you lost for words before, Chrissy," her aunt said gently.

"Did you do all this for me?" Chrissy asked in barely more than a whisper.

"Caroline did," her aunt said, glancing across with pride at her daughter.

Caroline walked toward her cousin. Her petticoats rustled beneath the pink-and-white gingham. "Happy Thanksgiving, Chrissy," she said.

Chapter 15

"Are you feeling as nervous as I am?"

"Nervous? I've got a whole herd of butterflies flapping around inside my stomach."

"Yours are only flying? Mine are stomping around with big hiking boots on!"

There was a general nervous giggle at this. Caroline stood in the wings beside the rest of the chorus girls, watching with interest. For the first time in her life she did not feel nervous. Excited, yes, but not the dreadful sinking feeling that the world would end if she made a mistake. Chrissy, as usual when she was nervous, was talking nonstop, asking the rest of the cast if they were as nervous as she was and dancing around so that her stiff underslips rustled. Caroline tapped her arm gently.

"Shh! You're making too much noise. The audience will hear you!"

"Audience!" Chrissy said in a whisper twice as loud as the rustling of her skirt. "Holy mazoley! Don't mention the word audience to me! I'll be fine as long as I don't start thinking about people out there waiting to watch me! Have you seen how many people there are out there? Hundreds and hundreds."

"I should hope so," Caroline said with a smile. "It wouldn't be much fun to go through all this for no audience."

Chrissy looked at her suspiciously. "It's all right for you. You've danced in public before. You've even danced for real audiences, not just parents and friends and students. But this is all new to me, and I'm so scared I can't stop my knees from knocking together. Do you think the audience can hear my knees knocking?"

Caroline giggled. "Perhaps they'll think it's the windmill creaking on the Oklahoma farm" she said, "and they'll say how very authentic the sound is." Seeing that Chrissy was not amused by this, she slipped an arm around her cousin's shoulder. "Just relax and tell yourself that you're going to enjoy every minute out there. You're going to be fine, and everyone is going to love your solo, and you'll get a big round of applause at the end of it, and they'll all say how funny you were and how well you danced."

Chrissy shrugged her shoulders in embarrassment. "Thanks, Cara," she said, "although I expect everyone will be watching you. They'll say that only one girl knew anything about dancing, and she made the rest of us look like elephants."

"You know that's not true," Caroline said warmly. "Now you'd better shut up because they're dimming the house lights, and that means no talking from now on."

Chrissy grabbed Caroline's arm in panic. "Don't let me do anything dumb, okay?" she pleaded. "Don't let me get caught in the curtains or fall over the light cables or forget to come off at the end of a number."

"I won't," Caroline said. "Just say to yourself that you're going to have a great time and that you'll remember this for the rest of your life."

"Okay," Chrissy said, giving Caroline her best beaming smile. "I'll try . . . I'm going to have a great time . . . I'm going to have a great time . . . I'm going to have . . ." She wandered to her starting position, and Caroline could see her mouth still chanting.

How funny she is, Caroline thought. *It seems really dumb to be scared of a little performance like this. Of course, it must be different if you've never danced in public before. I've already had my share of worrying and being scared. This performance is going to be different. There are no hard steps, no hard music cues, nobody is going to yell at me if my head wasn't turned right or my ankle wobbled on the arabesque. This is going to be nothing but fun!*

Caroline took up her opening position, ready to

run on to the stage with a covered basket over
her arm. The overture finished and the hero
strode on stage singing, "Oh What a Beautiful
Morning!" The song echoed what Caroline was
feeling. Life was pretty good. It was finally like
life should be—fun and relaxing, with no unbear-
able stress. The play had been fun all through
rehearsals, and nobody had minded too much if
anyone messed up. Even yesterday at the dress
rehearsal two of the boys had collided during the
Kansas City number and almost knocked each
other over. Everyone had laughed, including
Greg. "If that happens during a performance, act
like it's part of the routine," he'd said. "It's very
funny. Maybe we should keep it in."

"If we tried to bump into each other, we'd
probably miss," one of the boys said. "We'll have
to try and avoid each other!"

That was the atmosphere that Caroline enjoyed
so much—give and take between director and
cast, good-humored quips and nothing too serious. Caroline knew tonight that she should not
try too hard on stage. Her dancing should not
look too perfect compared to everyone else's. *I'm
just happy to be a chorus member,* she decided.

The song ended to a huge outburst of clapping.
The audience continued to laugh and applaud
right through the play, and after the *Oklahoma!*
finale, they stood and cheered. Caroline found
herself next to Chrissy as the cast gathered on
stage for the curtain call. She could feel Chrissy
trembling as the curtain rose and they stepped

forward.

"Holy cow!" Chrissy whispered, squeezing Caroline's hand. "This is the most exciting night of my life. Now I know why you like to dance so much. I want to be in every play that comes along after this. Do you think I should sign up for classes with Madame?"

Caroline shot her a horrified look as they dropped into a bow together. "Are you crazy?" she whispered. "After the first week one of you would be lying dead on the floor, and I'm not sure if it would be Madame or you."

Then the curtain fell and the cast walked quietly off stage before exploding with excitement. Flinging their arms around each other, they danced about screaming.

"We did it! We didn't mess up!" they sang out delightedly. "The audience loved it. Broadway, here we come!"

Caroline watched as the others celebrated. Although she'd had a wonderful time in the play, she shied away from the commotion and walked ahead toward the dressing room. Tonight her family was treating Chrissy to a very special dinner, and she wanted to be changed in a hurry.

As she turned into the darkened hallway behind the auditorium, she became aware of a figure standing in the shadows.

"Alex?" she asked uncertainly.

Alex was standing exactly as he had after her last dance performance, holding a spray of red roses. It was such an incredible touch of déjà vu that Caroline wondered for a moment if she'd conjured him up out of her memory. On the last occasion, he'd stepped forward and handed her the flowers shyly. This time he didn't move.

"Alex, what are you doing here?" Caroline asked, hearing her voice trembling. Inside her head a wild hope surged forth. He was going to hand her the flowers and tell her that he'd missed her and wanted her back again.

"Oh, hi, Caroline," he mumbled. "Nice show. Good dancing." The hand holding the flowers lowered awkwardly to his side. "I . . . er, was waiting for Jan. Is she about to come out, do you think?"

"Oh," Caroline said, coming down to reality with a bump. "Oh, Jan, yes, she should be out right away. She was just coming . . . I'd better be going."

Alex stepped forward and blocked her way. "How have you been doing, Cara?" he asked gently. "I think about you a lot."

"Not as much as about Jan, obviously," she said, and wished she hadn't.

Alex made an embarrassed face. "Right now Jan is the right person for me," he said. "We're having a good time together— but I do still think of you, Cara."

"You wonder if poor old Caroline is surviving and not dying of a broken heart?" she asked with a touch of sarcasm. "Well, don't worry, Alex. I'm doing just fine. I'm almost over you. I'm enjoying life, and things can only get better." Caroline dared to look him in the eye and was surprised when her heart did not start beating faster. She was just looking at a pleasant face with serious dark eyes. The nose was perhaps a little too big. She hadn't noticed that before.

Alex reached out and touched her arm. "I'd like us still to be friends, Cara," he said. "I've always enjoyed having you as a friend as well as a girlfriend. Maybe you'll feel like going out for a pepperoni pizza some day, just to talk. . . ."

"I'd like that, Alex," she said. "If Jan doesn't mind."

"Great," Alex said, then his face flushed scarlet as he looked down the hall. "Er, here she is now, Cara. I'll see you around, okay?"

"Sure, Alex," Caroline said. She turned back for just a second to watch him striding toward Jan, holding out the roses. She felt just one quick stab of pain as she turned back hastily and continued down the hall.

"Where are you off to in such a hurry?" Greg asked, stepping out from the lighting booth to intercept her. He loomed over her, so close she could smell the spicy scent of his after-shave.

"I just want to get out of here before the crush," she said, unnerved by his presence.

"Not hanging around to get your flowers and kisses?" he asked, his eyes teasing hers.

Caroline sighed. "Not hanging around to watch my ex-boyfriend give flowers and kisses to someone else."

"So that explains it," Greg said, resting one

hand easily on the wall to create a barrier in front of her.

"Explains what?"

"That quality you have—that remote look, the hint of suffering."

Caroline laughed. "You've been directing too many plays," she said. "That look was overwork and stress."

"It made you look very appealing and helpless, whatever it was, Greg said. "Did I ever mention that I go for helpless women?"

"I think you should know that I'm not all that helpless," Caroline said, gazing up at him, "and I'm not a woman yet either."

"I know," Greg said gently. "My worst luck. If I were a couple of years younger or you were a couple of years older, I'd ask you to have dinner with me tonight. I just wanted you to know that. Unfortunately I'm not a couple of years younger, and they'd never hire me to direct another high school play if I got the reputation for dating my students."

He smiled down at Caroline and she returned the smile. "Thanks for telling me, Greg," she said. "I want you to know that you did a lot for my ego when I was feeling very down."

"So the boyfriend breakup did affect you after all?"

Caroline nodded. "Pretty badly. It came at the worst time, when I was already about to crack under all that ballet pressure. I went around thinking that nothing good would ever happen to me again—that I'd never fall in love again—but you made me feel very special. I thought to myself, 'Cara, if a gorgeous guy like Greg notices you, then there's still hope.'"

"For Pete's sake, girl, you don't ever have to worry about getting guys to notice you," Greg said, shaking his head. "You're just one of those people who are a pleasure to watch. You'll be like the pied piper with a whole string of guys behind you by the time you go to college."

Caroline giggled to hide her embarrassment. "I wish," she said. "But one special one would be enough."

"That will come, too, I promise you," Greg said. "And if you don't have one by the time you start college, give me a call, if you'd like to date an old man of twenty-three."

"I think I might like that a lot," Caroline said, "if you're not in a wheelchair by then, that is."

"Caroline, are you down here?" Chrissy's voice rang out.

Caroline looked around guiltily. "I've got to go."

"Yeah, me, too," Greg agreed. "Take care, Cara." He put his finger under her chin and drew her gently toward him. Then his lips brushed her forehead before he hurried off in the other direction.

Chapter 16

"I couldn't eat another thing," Chrissy said, pushing her bowl away from her.

"That ought to go in the *Guiness Book of World Records*, Caroline teased from across the table. "The Great Wall Restaurant, only eating establishment to defeat Chrissy Madden."

Chrissy pulled a face at her. "You make it sound like I'm a real pig," she said. "I'm not that bad about food."

"Of course you're not, dear," Caroline's mother said hastily. "It's a pleasure to watch anybody enjoy food the way you do."

"And I really love Chinese," Chrissy said, looking wistfully at the food remaining on several platters. "It's just my stomach was so tense tonight, it won't stretch to its normal limits. It seems such a shame to leave those shrimps."

"We'll get the waiter to doggy-bag them for you," Caroline's father said. "Then you can have them for breakfast tomorrow."

"Daddy, don't be disgusting," Caroline said, wrinkling her nose. "Chinese food for breakfast?"

"It's what the Chinese eat all the time back in China," he reminded her. "Lots of good protein early in the day."

Caroline looked across at Chrissy. "I'll let you eat the leftover Chinese food," she said, "and I'll stick to my usual Sunday-morning croissant."

Chrissy smiled as she looked from one person to the next. "This was the perfect ending to a beautiful evening," she said. "I think it was the most exciting evening of my life. I'll have to write my folks the longest letter. . . ."

She paused and seemed to be staring past them to the carved pillar behind Caroline's head.

"Maybe you can teach me to cook Chinese food during the Christmas vacation," she went on awkwardly. "I'd like to be able to cook it for my family. There aren't even any restaurants that serve Chinese food like this back home. If you order Chinese, it's either chop suey or chow mein—maybe sweet and sour ribs, but that's definitely it. None of this delicious duck in plum sauce, or those little pork pancakes. What do you say, Cara—shall we do some experimenting during the vacation, get out recipe books from the library?"

Caroline hesitated. "Maybe," she said.

"I've got to keep myself real busy all vacation," Chrissy continued. I'm thinking of getting a job in one of the stores. Do you think they'll take me, even though I'm not sixteen until two weeks from now? I really want to earn enough money to go home in the spring—I don't think I could survive if I had to wait until June to see everyone again. I know I won't even recognize my little brothers. They'll have grown about a foot each."

"You mean they'll have three?" Caroline's father asked innocently.

Chrissy opened her mouth, then grinned. "You know what I mean," she said, laughing. "I mean that kids change so much around the ages of ten and twelve. I can't even picture them clearly anymore when I close my eyes. . . ."

Caroline touched her arm. "Do you think you could manage a fortune cookie?" she asked.

Chrissy looked down in surprise at her plate. "I didn't even notice them arriving," she said. "I have to make room for my fortune cookie, don't I? After all, there might be a terrific fortune waiting for me." She paused with the cookie unopened in her hand. "Have you ever noticed how there are never bad fortunes? Have you ever opened one and found 'You are going to have a rotten year'? or 'You have bad breath, don't open your mouth'?" She giggled.

"You might be the first," Caroline said impatiently. "Go on, open it."

The cookie cracked in two. Chrissy took out the slip of paper.

"Hey, this is interesting," she said. "GOOD NEWS IS WAITING FOR YOU VERY SOON! Hey, how about that! Maybe somebody saw me dancing tonight and wants to sign me up to be a showgirl in Las Vegas!"

Caroline looked across at her parents. "Can I tell her?" she asked quietly. "It does seem like the right time."

"Tell me what?" Chrissy asked.

Caroline's mother nodded. "Go ahead. It's fine with me."

"About the Christmas vacation, Chrissy," Caroline said. "We've made terrific plans! We were so sorry when it didn't work out for you to go home, we wanted to plan something really special. How does a trip to Southern California sound? We can visit Disneyland and Universal Studios and see Hollywood!"

Chrissy's eyes opened wide. "Disneyland?" she echoed. "I've always wanted to go to Disneyland!" She paused, then asked, "But won't that be very expensive for four of us?"

"It won't be too bad at all, Chrissy," Caroline's father said gently. "We'll drive down and stop at interesting places on the way, and once we get there, we'll stay with your aunt's old college roommate. That way the grown-ups can sit around and talk while you girls exhaust yourselves on Mount Everest or whatever it is."

"The Matterhorn, Daddy," Caroline corrected. "I have the strangest parents," she said, giving her father a withering look. "Can you believe they don't like things like Disneyland?"

"It's perfectly logical," her father said calmly. "I see no reason to pay in order to torture my stomach when I do not enjoy that sensation."

"There are other things beside roller coasters," Caroline reminded him. "All of Fantasyland."

Her father chuckled. "Can you see me in Alice in Wonderland's teacups?" he asked.

Caroline turned to Chrissy with a knowing look. "I'm so glad you're coming this time. My boring parents always leave me! It's not much fun on your own. I didn't even dare go on Space Mountain by myself—but with you, I'll try anything."

"I've never been on anything except the rides at the state fair," Chrissy said excitedly, "but I'm willing to try anything, too."

"Then that's all settled," Caroline's mother said with a smile. "You guys try everything and come home feeling sick, and we'll sit by the pool. Sounds good to me."

"Oh, wow, I can't wait," Chrissy said excitedly. "If you knew how much I dreamed of seeing places like Hollywood when I was a little kid. And can we drive around Beverly Hills and see where the stars live and look at the stores on Rodeo Drive? The kids at my school back home will be green with envy! We'd better take lots of pictures of me with Mickey Mouse and at the movie studios or they'll never believe me."

Caroline smiled to herself as she looked down at her plate. It was fun giving other people nice surprises. It would be lots of fun with Chrissy at Disneyland. In fact most things were fun when Chrissy was around. She felt a warm glow inside as she broke open her fortune cookie.

YOU ARE IN FOR SOME PLEASANT SURPRISES, it said. Caroline looked across at Chrissy crunching the last of her fortune cookie with a beaming smile on her face. *I've sure had enough surprises since Chrissy's been here*, she thought. *And I'm sure she'll give me plenty more before the year is over!*

Here's a sneak preview of *Dear Cousin*, book four in the continuing SUGAR & SPICE series from Ivy Books.

Dear Aunt Fanny,

I don't know what to do. I have a tremendous crush on a boy in my class. The problem is that I'm very shy. How do I let him know that I like him? I think he likes me a little, but he's kind of shy, too, and I'm afraid he'll run away if he thinks I'm chasing him. I'm so inexperienced in dealing with boys. Can you help? Please give me some advice on what to do next.

Signed,
Hopeful

Poor kid, I can understand just what she's going through, Chrissy thought as she stared at the letter. *It must be hard to talk to a boy if you are shy. I never felt shy when I was at home, but there have been lots of times since I came here that I wanted the ground to open up and swallow me because I felt so foolish.*

She stared at the letter again, feeling strangely uneasy about it. What was it about the letter that was worrying her? It was a perfectly normal sort of problem. It wasn't too serious, and Chrissy was pretty sure she could help. So why did she feel there was something strange about "Hopeful"'s letter? If only she could let Caroline in on her secret and talk things through with her, everything would be so much easier. Chrissy knew she wasn't the sort of person who normally kept things to herself. *I like to talk,* she thought. *I like to say what I'm feeling and thinking, not like Caroline, who . . .*

She stopped short and found her hand was trembling as she held the letter.

Could it possibly be? she asked herself. She got up and walked across to Caroline's desk, where she noticed some of Caroline's homework notes stuffed in her wastebasket. Chrissy straightened out the crumpled sheets and compared the handwriting to that in the letter. She couldn't believe her eyes—it was a perfect match!

Caroline wouldn't write a letter to Aunt Fanny, Chrissy thought, astonished by her discovery. *It's just not like her.* Chrissy remembered the conversation they'd had about Aunt Fanny with their friends. Caroline had asked if they thought people like themselves ever sent in letters, or just the weirdos.

But she has me, Chrissy thought helplessly. *She has good friends. She doesn't need an Aunt Fanny; she could have asked any of us for help. We'd all have been happy to put our heads together and come up with an answer. She shouldn't have to write a letter to the local agony columnist.*

She paused and gazed at her goldfish Elvis, swimming happily around his bowl. *I wonder who this guy is. Caroline has never even hinted that she liked somebody. How strange she is sometimes. When I had that crush on Hunter, the whole world knew about it!*

But Chrissy knew that Caroline did not find it easy to talk about personal things—that was why she had written to Aunt Fanny. She would never have guessed in a million years that Aunt Fanny was her own cousin.

Chrissy smiled to herself at the absurdity of the situation. Would Caroline find it funny if Chrissy told her the truth? Maybe she'd be glad to talk it over. Then they could plan a strategy to get this boy to notice her. It was such a nuisance that Chrissy had promised to keep her identity secret.

I'm going to do my best to help Cara with this, Chrissy resolved. *She needs a new boyfriend— she's been getting over Alex long enough. This new boy will be just the answer!*

Chrissy sat at her desk and took out a clean sheet of paper. What could she say that would help Caroline? What advice could she give? She could say all the standard things and tell Cara to act natural around him, to make a special effort to get to know him as a friend first by asking questions about his hobbies. But Chrissy got the feeling that this advice wouldn't be enough. She had seen Caroline around boys. Her cousin clammed up, opening her mouth only long enough for one-word answers that weren't likely to capture a boy's attention.

I get the feeling I'm going to have to do something more drastic in this case, Chrissy thought. *I'll set them up in a situation that throws*

*them together. Then Cara will have to say some-
thing, and he'll have to notice her. I remember I
did that for Margie Hamilton back home once . . .
let's see, what did I do then?*

She replayed the Margie Hamilton incident in
her mind. It had been a brilliant scheme, and
Chrissy smiled contentedly as she remembered
it. But her smile faded as she remembered the
ending of the scene: it had been such a fiasco
that Margie hadn't talked to her for a whole week
afterward.

So I wasn't too successful that time, Chrissy
admitted to herself. *But that was last year. I've
become more sophisticated living in the city. I'll
get Caroline together with her dream boy and she
won't even know that it's a setup. Maybe at a
party . . .*

ABOUT THE AUTHOR

Janet Quin-Harkin is the author of more than thirty books for young adults, including the best-selling *Ten-Boy Summer* and *On Our Own*, its sequel series. Ms. Quin-Harkin lives just outside of San Francisco with her husband, three teenage daughters; and one son.